Whispers of the Unveiled

A. HECATE KNEŽEVIĆ

Copyright © 2024 Arietta Knežević

All rights reserved.

ISBN: 9798329979572

DEDICATION

This book is dedicated to my mother, Karen, who has always encouraged my love of writing.

On a more facetious note, I'd also like to dedicate it to my guidance teacher from secondary school.

You gave me a detention in third year because you refused to believe that I wrote a poem in my notebook in my 15-minute break.

You said I must have spent an entire class period writing it, since, if I genuinely wrote it in 15 minutes, I'd have to be "a very talented writer". When I said I was, you laughed and said you'd look forward to reading my novel one day.

Well, here it is.

CONTENT WARNINGS

This book touches on some topics that may be sensitive.
If these themes are distressing to you, please ensure you have
access to the appropriate help before reading this book.

Potential triggers that may appear in this book are:

- Demons
- Death
- Violence
- Blood
- Fire
- Animal death (non-graphic)
- Pregnancy (brief mention)
- Body size/weight (descriptive)
- Child abuse (brief mention - implied)
- Sex (implied)

CONTENTS

Acknowledgements	i
CHAPTER ONE	p.1
CHAPTER TWO	p.14
CHAPTER THREE	p.27
CHAPTER FOUR	p.39
CHAPTER FIVE	p.49
CHAPTER SIX	p.60
CHAPTER SEVEN	p.75
CHAPTER EIGHT	p.86
CHAPTER NINE	p.100
CHAPTER TEN	p.114
CHAPTER ELEVEN	p.125
CHAPTER TWELVE	p.137
CHAPTER THIRTEEN	p.152
CHAPTER FOURTEEN	p.162
CHAPTER FIFTEEN	p.178
CHAPTER SIXTEEN	p.187
CHAPTER SEVENTEEN	p.199
CHAPTER EIGHTEEN	p.213
CHAPTER NINETEEN	p.221
CHAPTER TWENTY	p.230
CHAPTER TWENTY-ONE	p.240
CHAPTER TWENTY-TWO	p.252
Epilogue	p.261

ACKNOWLEDGMENTS

Thank you endlessly to:

Craig Williams, for designing the cover.

Obsidian Devnath, for editing and giving a wealth of advice on making the characters convincingly American.

New York City, for being such a magical and inspiring place that I couldn't come back and not write a book based there.

CHAPTER ONE

The simplest explanation is probably the right one. Occam's Razor - a principle that one small man in a big city stuck to all his life. Until he couldn't. Because it made sense. Until it didn't.

Cypress Rafferty was an aspiring artist. He'd packed his paints and brushes in one case and his paint-stained clothes in another and made his way from his family's Texas ranch to New York City. And like many aspiring artists in New York City, he quickly ended up spending less time painting than he did in a coffee shop just off Times Square, serving overpriced, overcomplicated coffee drinks to those who struck lucky where he didn't.

It was on his way home from that coffee shop, a cozy joint called "Pressed To Impress" surrounded by similar establishments with tired coffee pun names, that his life finally changed… though not quite in the way he'd hoped when he hopped off the plane three years before.

Walking through the lights of the square towards the

subway that would take him to the much less glamorous part of the city he called home, he paused. For a long time to come, he'd wish he didn't, but he did. He paused, his long dark hair becoming drenched by the spring rain, his eye caught by a face he'd seen on screens and newspapers: Eleanor Crouch.

She was a politician of some kind; he didn't remember. But he knew she was important. That wasn't what intrigued him, though: the real reason he faltered was that she was the second familiar face he'd seen in as many days at the same little stall.

On the corner of the street leading off the square, a tall, slim person with golden brown skin and a high ponytail dripping with beads had been peddling ornate silken scarves, dresses, and suits in vibrant colors for the past month or so. In that time, Cypress had spotted them with almost as many famous and significant people as he'd seen in the rest of his time in the city.

He made his way over to the stand opposite theirs, a small cart selling hot dogs and sodas from a mini fridge. "Howdy, Cowboy!" grinned the vendor, a short, stout man with graying hair and a mustache.

Cypress smiled weakly. It seemed like everyone who found out he was a Texan ranch kid made the same jokes at some point, and it was getting hard to continue acting like it was amusing. But today of all days, he couldn't tell Antonio where to go. He needed more than his occasional after-work snack.

"What's up, Tony? Just a hot dog with ketchup and

mustard, and a Coke."

Something about watching Antonio happily preparing his hot dog sent a pang of guilt into the younger man's stomach as if he knew he was about to pull him into something neither of them could yet fathom.

But he cleared his throat - *it's just a clothes stall, for heavens' sake* - and spoke.

"So, uh… the new guy. Or… lady? The new stall across the road. What do you think?"

"First of all, neither," shrugged Antonio. "They said they're a they-them, first one I ever met, so it took me a while! There's no they-them in Spanish. Even the wheels on this cart are female, you know? But it's all good. I get it now. It's called non-binary-"

Cypress took his hotdog from Antonio's outstretched hand, and jumped into the pause in his speech.

"So they're non-binary, okay. You don't have to explain that part," he chuckled. "That's not what I was curious about."

"Oh! You're asking about the woo-woo voodoo shit. Right."

It was said so matter-of-factly. As if he was talking about Tai's hair color. It caught Cypress off guard, and sent his first bite of hot dog down the wrong way, leaving him in a coughing fit and Antonio, having run from behind his cart, smacking his back.

After an excruciating few seconds that felt like a day, his breath returned, along with his ability to speak.

"I'm sorry, the *WHAT?!*" he hissed, his skin suddenly even paler than usual. "I was actually asking about the fact that politicians and B-listers seem to be regular customers, but never actually wear any of their stuff. Which is a shame, 'cause it's real nice, but that's not the point. If they ain't wearing the clothes, why are they hanging 'round Tai's stall?"

"The woo-woo voodoo shit, *manito*, I'm telling you," whispered Antonio.

This time, Cypress was expecting it, but it was still jarring to hear.

"What... woo-woo voodoo shit, Tony? What are you talking about?"

Antonio gestured with his hand, inviting Cypress to stand behind the cart under the canopy with him, out of the rain and the way of passing ears. His voice dropped to a barely audible murmur, but even so, his eyes darted around as if expecting Tai to appear and chide him for telling.

"Listen, Cowboy. Don't dig too deep into this. I don't know exactly what's going on, but I do know one thing - they're like, magical or something. I saw it with my own eyes, I swear. I heard of some stuff back in Puerto Rico, you know, Santería and stuff. But I never saw magic with my own eyes until that son-of-a-bitch showed up."

Antonio paused and furrowed his brow. "Son-of-a-bitch is

neutral. I think. It is to me."

Cypress nodded; that was dead last on his list of questions.

"Alright, but *what* did you see, bro?" he pressed.

"I'm getting to that part. 'Ey, eat your hot dog before it gets cold," said Antonio, clearly in no rush to get to the point. Cypress sighed and took a bite of the dog while the vendor continued his story.

"Okay, so when I first spoke to them, they said their name was Taina, but everyone calls them Tai. They said Taina means "secret" in some other language, I don't remember… but I asked them what the big secret is. I was just messing. They said *'it's not about my secrets, honey. Any secret, really. I can bring it to light, or make sure it never comes from under the rug. That's my thing'*".

Cypress raised an eyebrow. "The heck is that supposed to mean?"

"Well, that's what I asked," whispered Antonio, leaning in further, now almost touching Cypress' face. "They just smiled and offered me a scarf, saying the scarf can cover whatever you need it to, but it can easily be pulled off too. I said *'that's how scarves work, amigo'*. I took the scarf, I still got it at home, but I thought they were a little crazy, you know? Until I saw it for myself."

Patience was a virtue that Cypress felt he held in abundance, but in that moment, it was running thin.

"Antonio," he sighed, closing his eyes for a second to

regain composure. *"Please just tell me what you saw."*

"I'm getting there!" said Antonio, crossing his arms. "So, the first time, I thought it was just some strange coincidence. A couple walked up to their stall, and the guy took this blue scarf with butterflies on and was trying it on his girl, wrapping it around her neck, and putting it on her hair. Then Tai came and shook the scarf out, and put it over the girl's head, the couple were laughing, but Tai looked serious. It was covering her face, then her man pulled it off, right?"

Cypress nodded, intrigued.

"Suddenly he balls up the scarf and practically throws it at Tai. Starts yelling at the girl for sleeping with her boss. He runs off with her chasing after him crying, same show we see every day. But it came out of nowhere, and only after Tai covered her then she was uncovered… it was weird. Not weird enough for me to think too much about it, though."

"So there was something else?" asked Cypress.

"Damn right there was. You remember the guy who got shot down the road there, about two weeks ago?"

Cypress nodded. The whole street had been cordoned off, leaving him to take the long way to the subway station. By the time he got there, the train was abuzz with the breaking news - a woman had shot her partner fatally after finding out the devastating truth about his treatment of her seven-year-old daughter. She'd then followed up with another four rounds just to make sure - in broad daylight.

"I remember. Apparently he was a monster, so it's hard to have sympathy, but I hope the kid is okay. I'm glad she's safe now... but witnessing that? Damn."

Antonio nodded. *"Que atroz*. God bless her. But do you know how her mama found out?"

Cypress shook his head.

"That's the thing, no-one does. And rumor has it even the mama told the cops she doesn't know. But I saw it."

Cypress' eyes widened as he finally realized where this long and winding story was heading.

"The scarves?"

"The scarves, man. The kid walked over and was playing with this pink scarf, it was beautiful, and I guess mama was asking if she wanted it. The dude was there too, just hanging in the background. Then Tai came, and when they spoke to that kid... their face changed. I swear they knew, they saw something."

His breath caught in his throat, but he continued.

"They took the scarf from that little girl and they were messing around with it, showing how it fluttered in the wind and how big it was unfolded. Then suddenly it was over the kid... it covered her completely, touched the floor, and she was squealing inside, laughing. And then they told mama to find her."

"She took the scarf off... like the guy did with the cheatin'-

ass girlfriend? She uncovered her secret."

By this point, both men had tears welling in their eyes.

"You got it. Mama pulled the blanket off, laughing, then suddenly stopped. The kid was still laughing and begging her to buy the scarf, and she did. She bought it, and she wrapped it around the kid's head like a little babushka doll, and as she did, she was whispering something. The kid stopped smiling and looked terrified, and sad... I think that told that lady everything she needed to know. She reached into her handbag and... well, that was that."

Cypress drew in a long, jagged breath and swore, unsure what else to say.

"Thanks, Tony," he managed eventually, handing over a $20 note. "That's for the dog... the rest is a tip. Have a good day, my friend."

He didn't hear Antonio's reply. He was already making a beeline across the road towards silken scarves and gilded jackets.

When he approached, Tai was serving a middle-aged lady with her hair in a tight bun, and for a second, Cypress wondered if he'd overthought the whole thing and fallen into some kind of conspiracy theory.

Yes, Tai looked ethereal, and their side of the street somehow smelled of orange blossom, vanilla and musk with no hint of Antonio's hot dogs, car exhaust fumes or any of the other less aromatic scents of the city. Nonetheless, they still somehow seemed like a regular person running a regular stall.

The lady bought the red and gold scarf she'd been admiring, and Tai wished her a pleasant evening before turning to face Cypress.

"Goodness, honey, you look like a drowned rat," they grinned. Their accent was unidentifiable, almost like the transatlantic trill the women used in old Hollywood movies, but not quite. "Unfortunately I don't sell umbrellas - maybe I should, huh?"

Cypress fumbled for an answer, and settled for a nod and an awkward laugh.

"Is there anything you like the look of?" asked Tai, pulling a long emerald green scarf embroidered with tiny birds and leaves seemingly out of thin air. "I think this is your color. Careful not to get any paint on it, though - oil paints sure are a bitch to get out of fabrics."

They smiled in amusement as the man stumbled back a few steps.

"How did you-" he stammered.

"How did I know you paint with oils?" they grinned, winding the scarf around their hands hypnotically. "Well, I read your mind, sweetpea."

Seeing Cypress becoming even more flustered, they let out a light, chiming laugh.

"Calm down, honey, of course I didn't. What do you think

I am, a witch?"

Maybe.

"Well, maybe you do. But no, I just looked at you. You have some paint in the end of your hair, which could have been a coincidence, except that it's pure phthalo blue. Which means you didn't brush past something already painted, you got that from leaning over a palette. And it could have been someone else's palette, were it not for the spot of paint on the cuff of that jacket, probably from moving a painting that wasn't dry yet. The fact it wasn't dry yet means it wasn't acrylic, *that's* known for drying annoyingly quickly. Two plus two equals struggling oil artist."

Cypress stared in awe. *Maybe they weren't magical after all. Maybe they were just really, really observant.* Then he recalled Antonio's stories. No, there was definitely something more to this.

Realizing that he'd been staring and not speaking for far too long, he blurted out: "I'm not buying anything today. Just looking. I'm considering buying my girlfriend a scarf for her birthday next month."

"Ah, a fellow Gemini," smiled Tai. "I have one somewhere with the Gemini constellation embroidered on it. Let me know if and when you make up your mind - but I'd do it quickly, this is my last day in New York."

Street vendors pull that trick all the time.

'It's my last day, buy now', then they continue to show up

daily for the next several years.

But something told Cypress that Tai was for real; they didn't seem the type for cheap gimmicks.

"She's... not really a scarf kinda girl. I don't think I've ever seen her wear one," he said. It was true; Lani was a tattooed tomboy with her hair perpetually in cornrows, and her style was much more snapbacks and sneakers than silk scarves. *If it hadn't been true*, he realized, *he'd have never found the courage to say it.*

However, as soon as he'd said it, he realized that he'd shut the conversation down prematurely, so he threw the metaphorical hook back. "They are so beautiful, though! I'm still thinking of buying her one, just because." He made a point of feeling and looking through a few scarves before adding: "so, last day huh... are you going anywhere interesting now?"

"Everywhere I go is interesting, sweetpea," grinned Tai, before turning to attend to two teenage girls who were pawing matching floral peach-colored scarves that looked like Monet paintings.

One of the girls decided to buy both scarves, gifting one to her friend while they both promised to send their other friends the next day and "make these scarves trend."

As they babbled about wearing them on their social media feeds - *Hayley has five million followers, so your scarves are gonna blow up* - Tai laughed.

"As wonderful as that sounds, darlings, I won't be here

tomorrow. You'd have to send Hayley to Las Vegas. Now wouldn't that be fabulous?!"

The girls thanked Tai for the scarves and strutted away proudly wearing them, and Cypress fought the urge to literally jump for joy.

Las Vegas, eh? See you there, buddy.

Before Tai could turn their attention back to him, just in case they really could read his mind, Cypress walked briskly in the opposite direction from the girls, not sure where he was going until he realized that his feet were carrying him to his favorite bar.

A small Irish pub nestled between the flashing lights a stone's throw from Times Square, O'Rourke's had been his bolthole whenever he needed to compose himself before heading home.

Stepping into the low light of the bar, he felt the weight on his shoulders begin to lift instantly as 80s pop rock music replaced the bustling sounds and car horns of the city outside. It reminded him of the music his mother would listen to when he was a small boy helping her peel the bananas for her famous hummingbird cake. He took a deep breath, trying hard to center himself on that memory for a moment.

"What's going on, Cy?" asked the barman with a kind smile, and for a second, Cypress considered telling him. *Maybe it would help to say it all out loud*, he told himself. Then he realized that saying it all out loud would make it real, and hell, he didn't even know what "it" was yet.

"Long day at work," he shrugged. "I'll have a beer... and when I finish it, I'll have another."

"I got you," winked the barman, filling the glass from the tap before placing it in front of the wet and bedraggled man.

Cypress took a sip, if he could call it that - his "sip" drained half of the glass - and pulled out his phone. "I'm booking a flight for tomorrow morning," he said to no-one in particular.

"Work was that bad, huh?" called the barman while handing the woman at the other side of the bar something yellow in a martini glass.

"Something like that," sighed Cypress, realizing that he hadn't even considered work and making a mental note to call in sick from the airport. "I have something I have to do out there - in Vegas."

"Vegas? I never took you for a gambling man, Cy! Good luck, man."

"I'm not a gambler," he retorted. "But I think I'm gonna need that luck."

CHAPTER TWO

It's a five-hour flight from New York to Las Vegas, but for Cypress, it may as well have been a dream; a complete blank slate.

He knew he was waiting for his suitcase, but not what he'd packed from his haze the previous night. He barely even remembered leaving O'Rourke's at some indeterminate hour that now eluded him, let alone returning home and packing.

The fluorescent lights of the terminal cast a harsh glow on the scene, illuminating Cypress in stark detail. He was fully aware that he was getting a few curious glances from fellow travelers, and it came as no surprise; he could see in the reflective silver surface of the baggage carousel that his appearance was a study in dishevelment.

He was still clad in what was clearly the same plaid shirt and black jeans he'd worn yesterday, the fabric now crumpled and worn. His hair, unkempt and limp, framed a face marked by a shadow of stubble, teetering on the brink of becoming a full-fledged beard.

The slight gauntness of his cheeks and the faint circles under his eyes hinted at at least one rough night, and he could only hope that the people in the crowd around him assumed he'd been drunk or high. *God forbid they somehow knew the truth.*

As the carousel started up and hummed along, spitting out luggage with mechanical regularity, Cypress fought the urge to laugh at the utterly surreal detachment he felt from the throngs of mundane activity around him. The polished, sterile environment of the airport contrasted sharply with the shambles within him and the mysteries he now knew to be lurking outside.

Each suitcase that slid past seemed like a relic from another reality, a reminder of normalcy that felt just out of reach. Then, finally, his tattered green suitcase emerged, trundling towards him. He seized it with a sense of relief, the familiar weight grounding him momentarily, and made his way outside, hazel eyes squinting in the Nevada sun as he scanned the line of taxis.

He picked one at random and helped the driver load his suitcase into the trunk before jumping into the back seat on the opposite side from her, now overly aware that he hadn't changed, showered or used deodorant in far too long.

"Where you off to, New Yorker?" she smiled, taking a long drag of a watermelon-scented vape.

Cypress felt his chest tighten.

"How did you know I came from New York?" he asked, a little more aggressively than he'd planned. *"Who are you?"*

The blonde raised her eyebrows, looking back at him.

"Alright, let's get off the crazy train or we ain't going anywhere," she warned.

"I'm Bianca, I'm your driver, and I knew you came from New York because of the freakin' JFK tag on your bag. Is that alright?"

Feeling his cheeks flush, Cypress stammered out an apology, and the driver laughed.

"It's fine. You're not even the craziest one I've had in the car today, and it's barely noon. Now, can I ask where you're going, or is that classified too?"

"It's not, but you may think I'm even crazier... I don't know where I'm going."

The driver, whose name he now knew to be Bianca, shot another warning look over her shoulder.

"Listen, I'll pay whatever. And you'll get a hefty tip anyway, for putting up with me this far. How well do you know Vegas?"

She laughed out loud, as if it was the most ridiculous question she'd ever been asked, and took another drag, filling the car with watermelon-scented vapor again.

"I was born and raised in this place, and my father was a slot zombie who started taking me around all the best spots as soon as I turned twenty-one. If you're looking for the best casinos, I got you. And if you're looking for a whorehouse, I'll give you my ex-husband's number, I'm sure he got some recommendations for ya."

Choosing to ignore her final comment, Cypress explained: "I'm looking for a market stall."

"A market stall? What kinda market stall?" she asked. "Meter's already ticking, by the way, so I'd keep your story brief if I were you."

"If you were a street market vendor who'd been selling silk scarves near Times Square, where would you go in Vegas? What's the… equivalent?"

"Silk scarves? I'd bet on the Market in the Alley."

"Okay, great! Fantastic!" whooped Cypress, unable to conceal his relief. "Well, then I'm going to any motel near the Alley. That specific alley, I mean… the Market in the Alley."

Bianca started the engine, and, much to Cypress' gratitude, occupied herself with singing along to the radio for the rest of the drive there.

Just four or five power ballads later, they arrived at exactly the kind of establishment that springs to mind when you mention Las Vegas to someone who has never been there. A few palm trees dotted around the edges of the parking lot framed signs that, come dusk, would blaze with gaudy, flashing neon lights. An on-site wedding chapel completed the scene, embodying the quintessential vibe of the city.

After paying Bianca - with a generous tip as promised - Cypress removed his suitcase from the trunk of the taxi, offering the driver a nod as she sped off. The garish lights of the motel flickered above him as he approached the entrance. The lobby was dimly lit compared to the sun outside, and the air was thick with the scent of cheap perfume and potpourri, reminding him somewhat of his Mawmaw's house back in Amarillo.

A disinterested clerk with a gravity-defying teased beehive hairstyle and overfilled lips took his card. She handed him a key without a word outside of the usual script she now repeated mechanically, her eyes barely lifting from the magazine in front of her.

He trudged down the narrow hallway, the carpet worn and faded underfoot. The room number on the key matched the door halfway down. With a click and a creak, he was inside; the room was modest, with a bed covered in a brown and turquoise bedspread and a small TV perched on a dresser.

He dropped his suitcase by the door, headed straight to the bathroom, and showered until he felt clean, using all the provided shower gels. Wrapping himself in a worn, off-white towel, he returned to the room and sank onto the bed, the springs groaning beneath him. As he sat there, the weight of the journey finally settled over him, and for a moment, he simply breathed, gathering his thoughts, preparing for whatever came next.

After a few seconds, or maybe a few minutes, he grabbed the black landline phone from the desk to his left. "Do y'all have room service?" he asked before the clerk had a chance to say anything.

"We- yes, there should be a menu in your room, sir," she answered, clearly taken aback by his abruptness. "Is there something you need?"

Grabbing the menu from next to the phone, he mumbled an apology and rifled through it.

"Yup, I'll take the…" he allowed his eyes to scan the list of wines for a second - "the Prosecco? That's the cheapest wine, right?"

"Probably," she answered, her shrug almost audible over the phone. "Feel free to take your time looking to make sure. As it says right above the wine list, alcohol is only served from 5PM. It's currently 2:25PM."

"Listen, ma'am. I'm gonna need you to make a note, and add it to my tab at 5PM. Send it up to the room, or I'll come down there and explain to you why I need it, and then we're both gon' be drunk as two boiled owls come 5PM."

Silence greeted him from the other end of the line, and he wondered if she hung up, mentally scolding himself for the tone he'd taken with her. Then… "fine. I don't get paid enough to argue with you, or to give a shit what you do. Just don't advertise it."

A click denoted the end of the phonecall, and five minutes later, there was a knock at the door. He opened it to find the beehive-haired clerk holding a bottle of Prosecco in her hand, already uncorked.

"I couldn't ask room service to bring it, because I can't ring it up," she explained, handing it to Cypress.

"Thank you," he smiled weakly. "Sorry I was rude to you on the phone, I-"

"Save it," she replied, already on her way back to the front desk.

He considered going after her, but decided against it and retreated back to the bed with the bottle of Prosecco.

Taking a long swig, he felt the tension begin to melt away. Before he knew it, he had finished most of the bottle. The alcohol, coupled with his exhaustion, quickly took its toll and he fell asleep for the first time in days, still wrapped in his towel.

The next morning, he woke up groggy and disoriented, still hugging the mostly-empty Prosecco bottle.

"Dang it," he hissed in a moment of lucid realization, jumping out of bed and grabbing clothes from his bag, scrambling into them with no regard to whether his outfit (or even his socks) matched. *"The market..."*

He whirled through the free breakfast spread like a tornado, gulping down almost an entire jug of orange juice without noticing the indignant whines of the attendant and rushing out of the door with some kind of cheese pastry that he suspected may have been in competition with the nearby deserts for the driest thing in Las Vegas.

When he got to the market, he walked past the rows of stalls selling everything from paintings to jewelry to T-shirts emblazoned with obscure social media references he didn't understand. Dodging vendors calling out prices and parasols shading the walkway from the sun, he was looking for one stall and one stall only. And quicker than he expected, after turning a corner into the next row of stalls, he found it.

He smelled Tai before he saw them; that same intoxicating scent of orange blossom and sweets that he'd noticed back in Manhattan. Then, he saw the bright folds of silk and the curious figure swooping gracefully in and out of them, offering now an even larger selection of dresses, suits, and of course, their signature scarves.

Cypress felt grateful for the buzzing, vibrant hive of activity that enveloped him in the market - the colorful chaos made it far easier to stay under cover and out of Tai's attention than it was when he was hanging around their stall in New York.

Here, amidst the throngs of people flowing like a river through the narrow aisles, he could blend effortlessly into the waves of human movement. The crowd, enchanted by Tai's offerings and everything else around them, created a never-ending dance of bodies and colors.

In this hive of faces, a single bee buzzing through the masses, never lingering too long, would remain invisible unless he chose otherwise. It was comforting to Cypress, allowing him to be present without drawing Tai's attention; to observe without being observed.
As he observed, though, he began to wonder if he'd made

a huge mistake. He'd spent almost everything he made from the last painting he sold on flights, the motel, the taxi, the damn Prosecco... just to see this mystical Taina's magic abilities for himself. He recalled Tony's stories, and began to wonder if maybe the old man had lost his last marble - the Tai before him now was simply an eccentric yet charming person. Strikingly beautiful, perhaps, but otherwise perfectly normal, selling exquisite yet perfectly normal clothing and accessories.

No-one suddenly gained secret knowledge after trying on a scarf. No lives were saved, and none taken. Just a very pretty person and their very pretty scarves.

Maybe I should throw one of those scarves over my own head, Cypress thought to himself, *and pull it off again. See what this is all about once and for all.*

But it was too risky - if there really was something going on, and Tai recognized him from New York, they'd immediately know he was onto them, and he wasn't willing to find out what a witch, warlock or whatever they were would do to keep their secrets.

He realized in that moment that he wasn't even sure why he was so desperate to uncover the secret. It wasn't a matter of money or fame. He interrogated himself for a few minutes in his own mind - *are you sure it's not about money or fame? What else do I have to gain here? I'm not that kind of person, though. Am I?*

Leaning against a parasol a few stalls down from Tai's, he came to the conclusion that *he simply wanted to know.* Despite being raised as a Catholic by a half-Irish family in

Texas, he'd somehow made it out without even a belief in the one God his loved ones and their preachers declared to be true and ever-present. The tall tales in the Bible just never made sense to him. And more importantly, he'd resolved to never believe in anything he couldn't see with his own eyes. It always went without saying that this included magic - *which sane person over the age of ten believes in magic, anyway?*

But now, everything he thought he knew to be right and logical had been thrown into question by this one person and their darn scarves. But to believe it, and genuinely accept that there was more to the world than meets the eye, he had to see it. And some small part of him so desperately wanted to believe it.

So he stayed, and watched, and waited to see.

As closing time approached, Cypress shook his head at his own whimsy.

Of course it's not real.

Why would it be?

How did I even get dragged into believing that it was?!

He cast a glance over at Tai, who stepped behind the vibrant display of scarves and dresses and emerged not even ten seconds later. When they did, Cypress' heart stopped.

Seconds before, they'd been draped in silk robes, gold beads dripping from their ponytail and framing their face.

Now, their hair was secured in a tight bun with not a bead in sight, and they were dressed impeccably in a suit that Cypress knew must have cost twice his yearly income.

"What the..." he muttered under his breath.

There was simply no way for them to have changed so quickly, with a hair restyle and all, even if they'd had a team of stylists waiting in the wings.

Holy shit. This is real, isn't it? It's actually real.

Checking their watch, they pulled black curtains around the stall and secured them before walking away, talking quietly into a sleek black mobile phone.

Cypress set off behind them, following at a distance, but as he passed the now-closed stall, curiosity overtook him. Keeping one eye on Tai, he pushed a hand into a small gap between the curtains on the side, widening it just enough to peer through.

He was prepared for most things - magic lamps on a back shelf, dragons playing among the fabrics, maybe even a twin or replica of Tai, still in silk and beads, meditating in the space between the racks, levitating a few inches above the floor. From the anticlimactic to the downright absurd, his brain had already flooded with every possibility of what he might see through that gap... or so he thought.

What he actually saw made him stumble back from the stall, a hand clasped over his mouth, biting the palm - partly to stifle any uncontrollable shouts or swears but mostly to convince himself that he was, in fact, awake, and this was, at least to his knowledge, real life.

He took another peek, just to make sure, and walked away with his ears ringing, threading his way through the crowd, now even more determined to find out where Tai was going.

It took him too long to notice that his hands were shaking violently. He shoved them into the pockets of his white chinos in an attempt at feigning nonchalance, though sure that he'd never achieve anything close again. He'd been prepared for almost anything when he looked behind that curtain. But nothing could have prepared him for *nothing*.

All of the dresses, the suits, the scarves… gone.

It was, for all intents and purposes, an empty space.

Cypress closed his eyes for a split second, contemplating whether he should head back to New York and forget that any of this ever happened. New York, its familiarity and clockwork routine, seemed a million miles away, beckoning him back to a life he understood. But deep down, he knew he couldn't let this go now.

Seeing Tai change their entire look in a few seconds was one thing; he might have dismissed it as a trick of the mind, a symptom of jet lag, a hangover, or any other mundane explanation that allowed him to move on.

But the sight of the empty market stall had shattered any illusions of returning to normalcy. Cypress knew he was in this now, committed for the long haul.

Everything had changed forever in that fleeting moment, with that peek behind the curtain.

There was no turning back.

CHAPTER THREE

Tai's willowy frame vanished into the crowd, and Cypress quickened his pace, now wholly focused on trailing them and figuring out exactly what they were doing here.

To his surprise, instead of climbing into a sleek, opulent car he'd half expected to materialize from thin air, they slipped into the front seat of a taxi. Without missing a beat, Cypress darted across the parking lot and jumped into the backseat of the one behind.

As he settled into the worn leather seat, he still couldn't shake the surreal sensation that had washed over him when he looked behind the curtain. It was as if he had stepped into a scene from a film, the air thick with intrigue and the promise of revelation. Leaning forward, he locked eyes with the driver through the rearview mirror. "Follow that car," he told the man in a voice shakier than he'd hoped for, pointing at the white cab that was now pulling out onto the main road.

The driver raised an eyebrow but said nothing, the engine

roaring to life as their own taxi pulled into traffic, two cars behind Tai's.

Cypress felt a shiver of excitement run down his spine. He was no longer merely an observer in this unfolding drama; he was a participant, thrust into a role he had never imagined. The city blurred past him, the buildings and lights merging into a dizzying blur as the taxi kept pace with Tai's vehicle.

As they drove, Cypress was quiet, contemplating the many sticky situations he may be speeding directly into. What if Tai lived here, and they ended up outside his house? How would he explain that to the taxi driver, let alone Tai?

He was sure the driver heard his sigh of relief when, ten long and nerve-wracking minutes later, they pulled up outside a large and ornately decorated casino.

Of course they're a gambler. They know secrets, read minds, whatever... easy money. How did I not expect that?

"Uh, hello?" called the taxi driver, pulling the brake on his train of thought. "$11.47."

Cypress pushed a crumpled $10 and $5 into his hand and jumped out of the car, straightening his navy blue shirt before walking up the black marble stairs towards the gilded door.

Two titan-like security men, their skin almost as smooth and dark as the obsidian dragon sculptures around them, stood by the door in gold-trimmed white suits, framing it like bookends. Cypress tried his best to avoid their eyes—

or rather, their sunglasses—praying they'd overlook him. But there was no such luck.

"There's a dress code, bro," growled the taller of the two, looking over his shades. "You're supposed to wear a suit. Maybe the Big Booma down the road would be more your vibe?"

"Oh, gosh, I'm sorry!" replied Cypress with a sheepish smile. "But I came all the way from New York just to experience the Devas Casino" - *thank God I looked at the sign on the way in* - "so, is there any way you could make an exception for the dress code this once? I didn't bring a suit with me."

The second security man stepped forward, looking Cypress up and down like a cat surveying a mouse hanging from its claw.

"Armand owns most of the rest of the casinos in this part, anyway. Plus half of the strip. His name just ain't on 'em, but *technically* they're still Devas casinos."

"Armand?" asked Cypress inquisitively, immediately realizing that he may have made a mistake.

"Armand Devas. Of Devas Casino… and Devas Spiced Rum, if that's your poison."

Cypress slapped a hand to his head playfully, as if he couldn't believe he'd forgotten, with a laugh that came out a little too loud.

"Of course! I don't usually hear him called by his first

name, that's all. It's usually just 'Devas', you know?"

"Riiight..." nodded the bouncer, clearly unconvinced.

"Listen, man. It's been a long flight. And... my flight back is in the morning, so now I don't know what to do. I'm not with it."

The first bouncer, slightly taller yet marginally less menacing, stepped in front of him and looked down at Cypress.

"Not with it, and you're still showing up here hoping to gamble against the best? I admire your balls, dude. Look, just tuck in your shirt, put this on-" he produced a tie from his pocket, blue silk with white embroidered seagulls - "and stay out of trouble."

Cypress nodded, and thanked both men profusely. He tucked in his shirt as instructed, and began to put on the tie, but as he knotted it, blood rushed to his ears. Not only did the tie look strikingly like Tai's handiwork... the colors matched his outfit to perfection.

You're paranoid, he told himself as he strode inside. *It's just a coincidence. Why - HOW - would the bouncers at this fancy-ass casino be magical too? Get it together, Cy.*

He tried his best to cut a casual figure as he walked inside, knowing that showing even a hint of the amazement coursing through his mind and body would draw attention.

Black marble. Everywhere. Everything was gold-trimmed. Two golden chandeliers bigger than Cypress' studio apartment hung from the ceiling, dripping with gems and crystals of every color. *How is this real?*

He forced himself to tear his eyes from the glittering stones and scan the room to find the bar. As he sat down on a plush velvet barstool, a breathtakingly beautiful barmaid with seemingly endless curls of dark brown hair and a smile that reached her jade green eyes approached him. She was dressed in a white three-piece suit identical to the ones he saw on the security men outside, except she wore hers with gold kitten-heeled shoes, and a name tag on her left lapel engraved with "Kyra".

He'd fully intended to order a beer, but as he opened his mouth to do so, he realized how thirsty he was. After the full day standing in the heat, already hungover from the Prosecco last night, he accepted that (unless he was willing to risk the cleaning bill for throwing up all over this incredible place), more alcohol was not the best plan.

"I'll take a soda water and lime, please," he smiled, attempting to actively ignore Kyra's intense eye contact.

"With vodka or gin?" she grinned back, and he shook his head.

"Not today, ma'am. Just soda and lime."

She shrugged and prepared his drink, and after paying, he sipped it slowly while looking around the room, eyes searching for any sign of Tai. In their usual attire, Tai would have stood out like a vivid watercolor sunset against a white wall - a vision of bright robes and beads amidst a sea of black and blue suits. But tonight, they blended in seamlessly.

Cypress was close to admitting defeat and leaving when the spirit of luck in the casino decided to wash over him. From a side corridor, another white-suit-clad woman appeared, tall and blonde like a Swedish supermodel, pretty like a meadow where Kyra was pretty like a moonlit lagoon. She caught Cypress' eye, and he watched her as she crossed the room, making a beeline for a poker table in a booth near the corner.

She leaned down and whispered something to a tall figure with a slick bun, and Cypress quickly recognized that it was the very figure he'd been searching for. Tai stood up, and the blonde took their place at the table, allowing them to slip a white scarf around her shoulders as she did so. Tai then turned and walked briskly towards the corridor from which she had emerged.

"Hey, Kyra?" called Cypress, and the barmaid spun around, clearly surprised to have been called on by name. "I have to go to the restroom, would you just watch my drink?"

"Your drink's safe here, Hold'Em. But if it helps, I'll put it behind the bar 'til ya get back, alright?"

"Thank you. Wait, why are you calling me Hold'Em?" he asked, furrowing his brow in confusion.

"That's a Texan accent, right?" she asked, in the same tone a kindergarten teacher would use to explain something to a perpetually confused toddler. "So, you're from *Texas*, and you're in the *casino*. Texas Hold'Em!"

Cypress normally would have appreciated the joke and stayed to banter with her longer, but Tai had almost reached the entrance to the corridor, and he didn't want to lose them, so he laughed politely and nodded as he jumped up and started heading in the same direction.

"Hey, Hold'Em! Restrooms are that way!" he heard behind him, but he didn't look back. Maybe he'd explain to her later that he was in the middle of saving the casino from a witch... or maybe not.

His heart pounded as he followed them down the dimly-lit, quiet corridor, grateful for the plush black carpet muffling his footsteps. Tai soon made a right turn into another entrance, and Cypress crept up to it, smelling cigar smoke and hearing voices from within.

He pressed himself flat against the wall, listening carefully to the hushed tones.

He recognized Tai's voice first.

"You're here to siphon money from those who need it least. To do your bit to stop wealth screwing up the world any more than it already has. That's the point in this whole casino thing. Not to indulge your own vices - you're going to bring the whole thing down."

"Oh, do calm down," replied an unfamiliar voice with an audible smirk. "You mean to tell me you're playing completely by the book? Give me a break. You do your thing, and let me do mine."

"I know it's your *thing,* darling. I understand that. But with all of these women lurking around you all the time… it's a matter of time before one of them finds out something they shouldn't. Then we're all up shit creek, and when that happens, best believe I'm using your head as a paddle."

Cypress screwed his eyes closed, trying to work out exactly what he was hearing.

It's some sort of organized crime ring? The Mafia, or something? THAT explains the connections with powerful people…

Just as he started backing up, trying to process the fact that he'd followed a Mafia member to another state, let no one know where he was, and was now barely ten feet from a mob meeting, something crossed his mind.

The market stall.

Living in New York City and overhearing countless conversations on the subway every day had left him more than aware that the Mafia can make people disappear. But making an entire stall full of clothes disappear was even beyond their capabilities.

Part of him felt relief that he wasn't dealing with mobsters, but a much louder part was terrified, knowing that whatever he *was* dealing with could be far worse.

He shook his head as if to literally move the idea away, and refocused on the conversation.

"I don't care, Asmodeus," said Tai. "I know that it's your nature, but you have Succubi all over the damn place to take care of that. The one behind the bar is getting your clients left right and center, too, and do I say anything about that? No. But when there's women showing up at your house making a scene because you couldn't keep it in your pants, there's a problem. You're letting people get too close."

Cypress barely took in what was being said; he was still caught on one word: *Succubi.*

He knew they were sex demons that feed on men at night, but he didn't understand what that had to do with the women in white suits... especially Kyra. So what did Tai mean by Succubi?

Suddenly, he realized: *Escorts.*

That's why Kyra had been so flirtatious and friendly? She was a high-class escort? Damn.

He ignored the pang of disappointment, quickly followed by guilt, that hit him in the stomach upon this revelation.

The second voice, whom Tai had referred to as Asmodeus, let out a low chuckle. "How very rich of you to lecture me on allowing people to follow me and get too close, when there's someone lurking outside."

Shit.

Before Cypress could even process that thought, he was aware of Tai standing over him.

"And you are?" asked Tai pointedly.

"Yes, I'm- I'm only here for a few nights, I was looking for the restroom," babbled Cypress, resisting the urge to wipe his clammy hands on his pants.

Tai placed their hands on their hips and raised their eyebrows.

"I didn't ask what you're doing, dearie. I asked who you are."

Hearing this, a handsome man who looked to be in his early forties strolled leisurely out of the tiny private bar and stood beside Tai. He was slightly shorter than Tai, but still taller than Cypress, standing at around 5'10 not including his impossible quiff of wavy jet-black hair. He was dressed in a deep burgundy velvet suit over a black jacquard shirt, unbuttoned just enough to show a gold chain holding a pendant. The pendant was in the shape of a complex swirly symbol that Cypress didn't recognize, nestled in the man's chest hair.

He held a Cuban cigar in one hand and a mostly-empty whisky glass in the other, and amusement danced in his dark eyes.

"Well, you heard 'em," the man demanded. "Who are you?"

"My name is Cypress. Cypress Rafferty. I'm from-" he stopped himself before he could say New York, aware that it might set alarm bells ringing for Tai. "Texas. I'm from Amarillo, Texas. I'm just visiting for a few nights."
Tai extended a slender hand, which Cypress shook weakly.

"I'm Taina. It's a pleasure to meet you, Cypress Rafferty from Amarillo, Texas."

"You too," nodded Cypress, before extending his hand to the other man, who placed his cigar in his mouth in order to take it in a vice grip.

"I... overheard some of your conversation. I wasn't eavesdropping, just waiting for y'all to finish so I could ask for directions... but your name is Asmodeus, right? It's good to meet you too."

The man let go of Cypress' hand and let out a low, raspy laugh as he took the cigar from his mouth.

"Oh, that's just a nickname that my friend here gave me. I'm a simple man, Mr. Rafferty, I like racks on chicks and stacks of chips. You know? So they call me Asmodeus."

Cypress nodded, forcing a laugh. "Clever," he nodded, making a mental note to look up the name later so that he might understand the reference, unwilling to show that it was completely lost on him.

"My real name is Armand. Armand Devas. As in the Devas casino you're apparently exploring right now."

"And half of the rest of Las Vegas! Wow, it's an honor," remarked Cypress, recalling his earlier conversation with the security guards outside, and Devas chuckled in response, blowing out a ring of smoke.

"You flatter me. I like people who flatter me," he grinned. "If you're looking for the restroom, you're lost. Head back the way you came and past the bar. To the left of the slot machines, you'll find them. Pretty well signposted, or so I thought."

"My bad," smiled Cypress, already backing up. "I saw your friend come this way and assumed… yeah. I'll just…"

He allowed his voice to trail off as he turned and walked, controlling every step so that he didn't break into a run, back the way Devas had instructed him to go.

"What's up, Hold'Em? Still looking for the restroom? I can escort you…" trilled Kyra as he walked past the bar, but his head was spinning too fast to acknowledge her.

He stumbled into the restroom and looked at himself in the mirror, realizing just how much he stood out among the suited and booted bigwigs outside, and turned on the tap, splashing cold water onto his clammy face over the intricately carved snowflake obsidian sink.

Cypress stayed there for a few minutes, watching the water swirl down the drain, contemplating his next steps. Should he go back and get his drink back from Kyra, and wait for Tai to reappear? Should he sneak back to Devas' private lair and see if they're talking about him? Countless possibilities swirled down the drain with the water, as for the first time in days, Cypress chose the most sensible plan of action: *leave the casino, go back to the hotel, and get the hell out of Las Vegas as soon as possible.*

CHAPTER FOUR

After a flurry of desperate phone calls and a hastily concocted story about a family funeral, Cypress found himself booked on the red-eye flight to New York. The thought of staying another moment in the hotel was unbearable, so he made his way straight to the airport, grateful to be taking his last Las Vegas cab ride for what would preferably be a long, long time.

The terminal's endless stretch of identical burger joints greeted him with the comforting aroma of grilled meat, plastic cheese and fries. Choosing one at random, he ordered his first hot meal since that damn hot dog back in New York... if that could even be classified as a meal.

Settling into a plastic seat, Cypress pulled out his laptop. His fingers tapped frantically over the keyboard, punctuated by the occasional muttered curse, until he finally coaxed the airport WiFi into cooperating. As he waited for his order number to be called, he typed Armand Devas' name into the search engine, unsure what to expect. Somehow, after everything Cypress had witnessed and heard, the results were disappointing - it seemed Devas really was just a casino bigwig with a harem of girls working for him and a bigger harem of all genders on a rotation into his bed.

He'd founded his own brand of rum, flavored with vanilla and cinnamon and spiced with ghost chillies, five years ago.

He boasted six high-profile engagements, none of which made it down the aisle.

And he'd been cautioned by the police when one of his pet American crocodiles made it out of his private lake and off the vast expanse of his property, causing a half hour of chaos and (allegedly) a missing Chihuahua.

Some of the reports about the crocodile incident claimed that Devas had shown up on the scene and whistled the 17ft reptile to heel like a well-trained dog before leading it back to the grounds of his palatial mansion. But beyond that, he seemed like a fairly ordinary, albeit rich and obnoxious, man.

As Cypress scrolled, he remembered something: the nickname Tai had given Devas. *What was that all about, anyway?*

He typed slowly, trying to figure out how it might be spelled.

A-S-M-O-D- *Asmodeus.*

It appeared in the suggested search bar, and Cypress

clicked on it immediately, but at the same moment a cashier called out number 239, indicating that it was time for him to pick up his food from the counter.

He carefully carried his tray back to his seat to avoid spilling his sweet tea, and sat back down. As he took a huge bite of the chicken sandwich he'd had loaded with bacon, ranch and a frankly unreasonable number of grilled bell peppers, his eyes finally settled back on the screen.

The first thing that caught his eye was the same swirly symbol he'd seen on Devas' gold chain.

He could study it better now, and it looked like a twisting, almost serpentine letter D, with a devil's tail.

It must have been a gift from Tai, Cypress realized. *A necklace symbolizing his nickname.*

Shoving a few crispy, salty fries into his mouth, Cypress wiped the sauce and grease from his fingers with a thin paper napkin before clicking on the first result to read more about Asmodeus.

One of the nine Kings of Hell, King Asmodeus was a high-ranking demon, and a patron of all flavors of debauchery.

"King Asmodeus, also known as Asmodai, is a formidable figure in demonology, often associated with lust and gambling. His influence extends over carnal desires and the temptation of games of chance, making him a patron of both vice and risky pleasures."

"In many depictions, Asmodeus is shown riding a giant

crocodile, symbolizing his dominion over primal and predatory instincts."

"This demon king's allure is as powerful as it is dangerous, drawing individuals into a web of sinful indulgence and reckless wagers."

As Cypress read article after article, a cold feeling settled over him. The sex and gambling would have been one thing. The necklace may have been a gift related to those similarities. But the crocodile story needled in the back of Cypress' mind, a nagging voice saying that it seemed like more than a humorous coincidence. And given that there was no more room for doubt in Cypress' mind that Tai had some kind of otherworldly powers, he found himself quickly becoming increasingly convinced that Armand Devas was King Asmodeus himself.

Asmodeus owning half of Las Vegas wouldn't just make sense, it would be almost ridiculously on-brand. And while researching the demon king, he'd quickly found out about a practice called demonolatry; the practice of worshiping and venerating demons through rituals and invocations, treating them as powerful spiritual guides rather than mere symbols of evil. He learned how the practitioners believe in forging relationships with these ancient beings, seeking their guidance, wisdom, and power. And slowly, everything started to make sense in his spinning mind.

Maybe Tai isn't a witch. Maybe they're a demonola- demonolotrist?- demon worker. And maybe all that power is actually Asmodeus'.

He copied everything he could find on demonolatry into

blank documents on his laptop, preparing to spend the flight home combing through every detail, determined to figure out exactly how this worked and what Tai was up to.

But by the time his flight landed, the only thing he'd figured out was that most practitioners have one entity that they're closest with, but rarely do they only work with one… and *that* meant he'd barely seen the tip of the iceberg.

Unwilling to waste any more time, he headed straight from the airport to the library, suitcase still in tow, laptop bag hanging from his shoulder, arriving there just minutes after opening time.

"I need everything you have on demons," he told the librarian, a portly woman with her silver hair neatly pinned back and a delicate Star of David pendant resting on her chest. She exuded a calm authority that made him instantly regret his abruptness, and her raised eyebrows and pursed lips suggested he might have been wise to at least say hello first.

"Sorry," he grimaced, taking a deep breath before starting again. "Do you happen to know if you have any books on demonolatry? Demons? Ars Goetia?"

Aware that he was now just parroting words he'd picked up from his unconventional in-flight reading, he stopped and smiled politely at the librarian. "Please?"

She sighed, looking over her glasses at the computer screen as she typed.

"This is everything we have," she told him as the small printer next to her whirred. It produced a slip of paper and she handed it to him; a list of titles accompanied by the shelves on which he could find them.

Forty-five minutes later, Cypress reappeared in front of the librarian, looking slightly disheveled but triumphant, his arms laden with a precarious stack of books. She had allowed him to leave his suitcase by her desk, and it now served as a silent witness to his frenzied search through the library.

The titles he carried ranged from ancient grimoires to modern studies on demonology, their worn spines and dusty covers promising a wealth of arcane knowledge. As he set the pile down with a soft thud, the librarian's curious gaze followed him, her earlier skepticism giving way to a hint of curiosity.

"Are you checking all of these out?" she asked, and Cypress was about to answer in the affirmative when he stopped himself. Looking through all of these and finding everything he had to know could take much longer than the two weeks the library allowed, and he'd rather not keep lugging them back across town to renew them.

"Actually, how much does it cost to use y'all's photocopier?"

Her eyebrows shot up into the stratosphere again as she looked at the pile of books in front of her.

"Each page is twenty-five cents. You'd probably be better

off buying the books, kid."

"Oh, I'm not copying everything," he promised, before taking the books over to the large white machine on the other side of her desk and starting to rifle through them.

Page after page fluttered out of the copier - summaries of the characteristics of each demon, their roles in mythology, their roles in practitioners' lives, sigils and offerings and how to invoke them...

"HEY!" yelled the librarian, pulling Cypress' attention away from the reams of paper for a second. "Are you kidding me? If you bust the printer, you'll be the one replacing it!"

Cypress stammered an apology, gathering up his copies and stacking the books back into a pile.

"Should I put the books back?" he asked, and the woman shook her head.

"You're good, just put them on that cart over there and Asher will put them back at closing time."

Feeling a twinge of sympathy for whoever Asher was, he placed the books neatly into the cart before taking the copied pages to the librarian.

As she flicked through, counting under her breath, she shot the occasional death glare at Cypress, who met it each time with a sympathetic smile. Eventually, she slipped the papers into a bag typically meant for carrying books, and looked up at him.

"That'll be ninety-five dollars and twenty-five cents. And I gotta ask, kid: is there a reason you ran in here, clearly straight off the plane from Dustball, Arizona, and spent damn near a hundred dollars on... this stuff?"

Cypress laughed nervously.

"I'll give you a hundred, you can keep the change for your trouble."

The woman let out a goose-like honk of laughter, crossing her arms in disbelief.

"Well, ain't you generous? A whole four dollars seventy-five for having to count a buttload of sheets about demons and probably refill the ink cartridges."

"Sorry," he winced. "I didn't mean- look, that's all I have right now. I'm sorry. To answer your question, I left Dustball, *Texas* a few years back. I live here now. I actually got off the plane from Las Vegas. And there's no important reason, just research."

"Research? Research for what?!" she pressed, rubbing the pendant on her necklace between her finger and thumb as if silently calling for divine intervention, clearly feeling unnerved and intrigued in equal measures by the subject matter.

"A movie. I work in film production."

He mentally high-fived himself for the quick lie, and handed the woman her money in a jumble of notes and coins.

"Good luck with your movie, then," she said, handing him the bag of papers with an almost imperceptible head shake. "Don't forget your trunk."

Cypress thanked her once again, gathered up his things and headed towards the subway station, bound for home.

When he got there, every fiber of his body screamed at him to order a pizza and go to sleep, come back to this the next day. But his brain said otherwise.

Sitting on the paint-splattered floor of his studio, he laid out the papers in front of him and took a highlighter to every sentence about King Asmodeus, adding up all of the evidence he could find against Armand Devas. He flipped one page over and started scrawling on the back in green marker:

TAINA = DEMONOLATOR

ARMAND DEVAS = ASMODEUS

Two puzzle pieces of a puzzle bigger than he ever could have imagined. And he knew he couldn't stop there.

More names joined the list, some annotated with question marks, others scored out as new evidence came to light, and when Cypress' eyes tired of perusing the grainy words on the paper, he turned to his laptop.

With a quick search, he located a lengthy video delving into the lore of the demon kings. Clicking play, he sat poised, ready to transcribe every detail that could help him understand. Within a few seconds, however, he heard something that made him lose his grip on his pen, letting it clatter to the floor.

"First up, let's talk about King Belial, the Lord of Lies."

He'd read the name numerous times already, but apparently, in his head, he'd been pronouncing it wrongly.

He'd assumed the name was pronounced something like *"belly-all."*

But in the video, they'd pronounced it *"bell-isle."*

Hands shaking, he picked up the pen from the floor and added another name to his list.

MATT BELLISLE = BELIAL.

CHAPTER FIVE

Just sixteen blocks away, in a skyscraper overlooking Times Square, the media mogul known for controlling most of the news in (and perhaps outside of) the United States buried his shaven head in his hands.

"Look, Andras..." he sighed, but was interrupted by the short, muscular blond man standing in front of him, rounded face contorted in distaste.

"It's Bill."

Matt Bellisle was a foot taller, slender, with striking dark blue-green eyes. He looked down at his friend, shaking his head before rolling his eyes.

"Your name is Andras."

The shorter man smirked, showing sharp, almost fang-like teeth.

"Well, yes, but you changed yours too... twice!

Matanbuchus to Belial to Matt Bellisle. Humor me, man, come on. I put *so much thought* into my name!"

"Sure. The most basic name of all time, but yeah. It's genius."

Bellisle's antipathy was audible, and it was being taken none too kindly by the other man.

"Where do I live?" he asked, arms crossed.

"Buffalo," groaned Bellisle.

"Right! Buffalo Bill! And what am I?"

"An insufferable bin-juice drinking gronk."

Bill stamped a foot on the ground, growling in indignance.

"No, Bozo. I mean when we're not using these stupid glamours."

Momentarily, the man's visage transformed, revealing the head of a barn owl on what could only be described as the oiled shirtless body of a man with an intensive bodybuilding regime.

He switched back just as quickly, grinning at Bellisle.

"I'm a freakin' *bird*, man. I got a beak. Or in other words…"

"A bill," droned Bellisle, having heard this logic countless times already.

"See? It *is* genius. I'd appreciate if you recognized that and actually used it."

"Fine," snapped Bellisle. "Bill-"

"Thanks Bel," the shorter man chirruped, grinning ear to ear.

Bellisle took a deep breath, trying hard not to show how effectively Bill was rattling his cage. "I told you not to call me that. How many times did I tell you not to call me that? If I can call you Bill, you can call me Matt, Matanbuchus, Belial, Mr. Bellisle… take your pick. But stop calling me Bel."

"Bill and Bel… I think it's cute!" mocked Bill, forming a heart shape with his hands and finally tipping Bellisle's patience over the edge.

The taller man grabbed him by the collar of his maroon polo shirt, lifting him up to eye level as he struggled to reach the ground again with his feet.

"I don't," he snarled. "And what I especially don't find cute is you going around carving people up."

He opened his hand, letting Bill unceremoniously thud to the ground, stumbling as he landed.

"Belial, are you sure you know who I am?" laughed Bill.

"Making humans into hashtags is kinda my thing. That's why I'm here."

"I'm well aware of why the Emperor has you here, other than to be a pain in my ass," Belial continued. "You're here to get rid of the ones who are... a problem. But you have ways to do that - car crashes, illness, bridges falling down, shit, show up and do the Mothman thing in their room in the middle of the night, that's bound to cause a few heart attacks. But you can't keep doing it like this."

"How did you know I was Mothman?" cried Bill in mock defiance. "I thought I had the Hannah Montana double life thing down."

"I saw one picture, idiot. And you're completely skipping over the point."

Bellisle reached into his desk and pulled out an envelope.

"Chief of NYPD sent me these. I paid him under the table and told him it was to inform the stories - stories, by the way, that I'm suppressing to save your ass."

He tipped out the contents of the envelope onto the desk, and Bill saw that they were photographs. Crime scene photographs, to be specific. Bill smirked as he pushed them around, looking upon the gruesome images of artistic scenes made out of grotesquely mutilated human bodies.

"I fail to see the amusing side, Bill," Bellisle warned, making air quotes with his long, elegant fingers at the mention of his companion's pseudonym. "I mean it. You cannot keep doing this."

Bill ran a hand through his short blond hair with a dark

chuckle before looking Bellisle straight in the eyes.
"Oh, but I can, Bel. These pictures are proof that I did. If you remember, my plan was to just say fuck 'em and let them tear themselves apart. But then the big guy insisted, and you insisted, that we had to be here and do this. He told me I had to help, *you* told me that you needed my help. So here I am, helping… and *I did it my way!*"

Bellisle clenched his teeth as Bill burst into song with a flourish and a showman's grin. "Well, your way is insane. And it's causing problems for me, for the Emperor and for the whole plan."

"What's the big guy saying? Too much blood? Too many tears?" asked Bill with a mocking wide-eyed frown.

"You might want to start showing the boss some respect, Andras," chided Bellisle. "And he's less concerned about the blood and suffering - although that is its own issue - and more worried about the rumors. They think you're a serial killer."

"Do they also think the Pope's a Catholic?"

"I'm serious," growled the taller man, a warning hand taking hold of Bill's, or rather Andras', shirt collar once again. "There's some TV show that the people liked a while ago. There's a serial killer on there, and they call them the Eat The Rich Killer, because they go around killing off all these rich and powerful types. Given the… primary demographics of the people you're supposed to take care of, and the ways in which you choose to do so, there are rumors of a real-life Eat The Rich Killer."
"Well, that's bullcrap. I don't eat 'em," shrugged Bill.

"Too much fat on most of 'em anyway, and who knows what kinda drugs are in the rest."

"That. Is. Not. The. Point."

Each word from Bellisle was punctuated by a thump of his fist on the wall behind the other man, who smiled up at him, completely unthreatened.

As Bellisle measured what to do next, seriously considering opening the window of the 33rd floor office they currently stood in and finding out if a certain bird could still fly, there was a soft, almost hesitant knock at the door.

Bellisle stepped back, clearing his throat, and called for whoever was knocking to enter. The door opened, revealing a girl in her late teens who Bellisle recognized as Camilla, a journalism student and intern of his company.

"Mr Bellisle," she smiled apologetically, before noticing Bill leaning against the wall he'd been backed up to just a few seconds previously. "And Mr. Anderson - hello!"

"I was just leaving," said Bill, his voice suddenly much softer and sweeter, which conveyed a sense of danger far more insidious than any yell or curse. Camilla couldn't pinpoint why a primal fight or flight instinct was triggered deep down in her by this man, who was barely taller than her and never anything but polite, but she couldn't deny the wave of relief that washed over her as he disappeared down the corridor.

"I'm sorry if I interrupted anything," she mumbled,

fidgeting with the thick waves of her shoulder-length hair, which was dyed a dreamy shade of pastel pink. "I just, um, need to tell you something…"

"First of all, Miss Jenkins, I've told you before: you're under my wing while you're here," Bellisle said gently. "Bill - Mr. Anderson - very much has his own wings, and knows how to use them. So, don't apologize for interrupting. Anyway, you may have saved my sanity or his life, so yay you, I suppose."

The girl was confused but smiled and nodded anyway as Bellisle continued.

"Secondly… what was it you wanted to tell me?"

"Oh, right, yes, that," stammered a flustered Camilla. "Well, there's a guy outside. I think he must have something to do with the B.E.M campaign."

Bellisle sighed, cursing under his breath. Brett Edwards-Miller, a particularly smarmy election candidate, had been exposed for having an affair with a singer half his age. His wife, as a consequence, very publicly divorced him, his chances of becoming President effectively disappearing out of the door along with her.

Instead of taking any semblance of responsibility for his actions, Edwards-Miller, known in media circles as B.E.M, had squarely placed the blame on what he called "the lying, corrupt media," specifically naming Matt Bellisle at every opportunity he got.

"What are they doing this time?" he asked, and Camilla

pulled out her company-issued phone, her fingers dancing across the small screen until a live feed of the building's security cameras appeared.

She used two fingers, adorned with glittering pink nails, to zoom in until the figure outside was visible, and after a few seconds, Bellisle was able to read the message daubed on the huge canvas board the lone protestor was holding.

BELLISLE: LORD OF LIES.

Bellisle's eyes widened for a second, then he grabbed the phone and closed the feed.

"I've seen enough," he said, and Camilla nodded, about to apologize and leave, when he spoke again.

"Send him up."

Camilla stopped in her tracks and looked up into his eyes.

"Sorry, what?" she asked, her brow wrinkling.

"I don't recall stuttering, Miss Jenkins. Go, catch an elevator down there, tell the guy I want to talk and send him up. Escort him if necessary."

"But Mr. Bellisle-" she started, but Bellisle silenced her with a hand in the air.

"Before he gets bored and leaves, I am asking you once again to get your cotton candy ass down there and send him up."
The girl was taken aback by the sudden, and to her

knowledge uncharacteristic, change of attitude in her boss. He'd always been kind, with all the firm but fair authority of a high school principal. It was unlike him to take a swipe at her appearance - she'd have expected it from Bill, but Mr. Bellisle had commented more than once on how her love of all things pink brightened the overwhelmingly gray building and therefore his day.

She couldn't fathom what it was about this specific protestor that had managed to faze Bellisle so easily, especially when she exited the building and came face to face with him. He didn't look like much; just a short, slim hipster in his late twenties, sporting long dark hair and a yellow plaid shirt, with the haggard look of someone who hadn't slept in a week.

As she approached him, the man locked eyes with her. "Do you work for him? Matt Bellisle?" he asked.

"As a matter of fact, yes," she replied. "Well, kinda. I'm an intern. But he sent me down here himself."

"Well, I'm sorry, but I'm gonna have to send you back up to tell him I'm going nowhere," the man retorted, pointedly holding his sign up to face a security camera again. "Tell him my name is Cypress Rafferty, and I need to talk to him. I'll wait here until he leaves if I have to."

"I do most of the monitoring on those cameras at the moment, so that's useless," Camilla told him, gesturing to the sign. "And anything you have to say to Mr. Bellisle, you can say yourself. If you'd let me finish, that's what I wanted to tell you - he sent me down here to bring you to him. Apparently he wants to talk, too."

"Wait... *really?*" asked a wide-eyed Cypress, clearly not having expected to get this far.

"Trust me, I don't get it, either. You're the third person protesting about the Edwards-Miller exposé this week, and you didn't even try to storm into the building or throw paintballs like the other two. But he insisted on meeting you, and he doesn't seem to be feeling all too patient, so I suggest we go. And I suggest even more strongly that you leave the sign outside."

Placing the canvas board down outside the door, he followed the girl straight past the front desk and into an elevator. She pushed the button engraved with the number 49, and they started to ascend without a word between them, Camilla looking bored, Cypress' heart rate rising along with the numbers as they got closer to Bellisle's floor.

When the doors opened, Camilla pointed him towards a large black door adorned with a golden plaque reading *BELLISLE* in what looked like an old Celtic font. "Good luck, Mr. Rafferty," she called with a hint of amusement as the mechanical doors closed on her and he was left alone, staring at the door, wondering if he should knock or run back to the elevator, hopefully catching the pink girl downstairs and begging her to let him out again.

The choice was yanked abruptly out of his hands when the door opened, revealing Matt Bellisle. The man was even taller than Cypress had expected, and more elegant than he appeared on television and in pictures. His disarming good looks and slightly lopsided smile gave him a beguiling charm that made Cypress momentarily forget just how much danger he could be in.

"Hello, Mr. Rafferty," greeted Bellisle, extending his hand.

Cypress told himself that the girl must have already called to brief Bellisle on his name, but deep down, he knew she hadn't needed to. He hesitated for a second before accepting the handshake, and looked up at the man before him, meeting his eye for the first time.

"Hello, Mr. Bellisle. Or should I say *King Belial?*"

CHAPTER SIX

At the mention of his title, Belial grabbed Cypress by the arm with a vice grip and yanked him through the door into his office. The abrupt transition left Cypress momentarily off balance, and he stumbled slightly as he was propelled into the room.

Once inside, Cypress couldn't help but marvel at the sight that greeted him. He'd expected black marble and opulence like Asmodeus' casino, or maybe a simple, sterile corporate office, but the room was a verdant sanctuary, teeming with life.

Dozens of plants sat in variously sized terracotta pots scattered around the space, their vibrant green leaves creating a lush canopy. Vines and ferns climbed the walls and twisted around the legs of the mahogany desk, giving the office the look and ambience of an enchanted rainforest straight out of a fairytale.

Sunlight streamed through the large windows, casting dappled shadows across the floor and illuminating the room with a warm, golden glow. The air was thick with the earthy scent of soil and the faint, sweet fragrance of blooming flowers. It was a stark contrast to the concrete jungle outside, and as he stood there, momentarily captivated by the natural beauty surrounding him, Cypress could once again almost forget the perilous situation he was in.

Yet, the firm grip Belial still had on his arm was a constant reminder of the risks that lurked just beneath the surface of the tranquil facade.

As he closed and locked the door behind them, Belial finally released his grip and gestured for Cypress to take a seat in a corner armchair next to a large monstera plant.

"Would you like something to drink?" he asked. "A coffee, maybe?"

Cypress watched Bellisle fill his own espresso glass with coffee from a small silver machine perched on his desk, and nodded. "That would be great, thank you. I'll take it with oat milk and brown sugar, if you have-"

"You'll take it with rum," Bellisle interrupted without missing a beat, liberally splashing amber-toned liquid from a half-empty bottle labeled 'Devas' into a second glass of black coffee.

"Rum works too," laughed Cypress, but the sound was strained and he prayed that his nerves wouldn't betray him.

With pleasantries over, Belial settled into his own chair behind his desk and looked over at Cypress, eyes roaming up to his tousled hair and back down to his high-top sneakers like a lion surveying an unfortunate antelope.

"I must say," mused Belial, taking a slow sip of his rum-laced coffee, "I always knew this day could come. I'm not a reckless man, I never thought this was foolproof. But I always expected it to be some big drama, with some religious big shot. I never expected... well, *you*."

"I didn't expect it to be me, either," Cypress cried out, laughing in disbelief as he pulled at his hair. "I'm not... I'm just an artist. I pay the bills working at a coffee shop, and everything else by selling paintings in the square or at art fairs and... damnit, this is all insane! But now that I know, I can't just leave it!"

A half-smile graced Belial's face as he listened to the man ramble.

"And how exactly *do* you know?"

Cypress stopped babbling and looked over at Belial, who was refilling his coffee and rum.

"What do you mean?"

"Exactly what I said, Mr. Rafferty. You don't strike me as the demon-slayer type. So how did we get here?"

Cypress sighed deeply. "Curiosity killed the cat, I guess. All nine lives at once, let me tell ya."

A large, glossy leaf of the monstera beside him seemed to bend down and lightly settled on his shoulder, as if offering a gesture of consolation. Cypress glanced at the leaf, its rich green hue striking against the worn fabric of his shirt. He patted it appreciatively, feeling an odd sense of comfort from the plant's almost human touch.

In the increasingly ethereal world he found himself in, he was no longer sure what to consider mundane. In this space especially, every detail seemed imbued with meaning, every rustle of a leaf and flicker of light teasing a peek into a larger, incomprehensible narrative. He couldn't help but wonder what other secrets lay hidden in the lush depths of Belial's office, and whether he was prepared to risk finding out by entering this conversation with the demon.

The demon.

The thought rang shrilly in Cypress' mind, sending it spinning once again. Barely more than seventy-two hours ago, he was just another commuter downstairs, grabbing a hot dog on his way home from work. And now, he found himself in a jungle-office with a demon king. Reasoning that there was no way back to the status quo from this point, no matter what he said, he took his coffee like a shot, trying hard not to show how much the intense heat of the spiced rum fazed him.

Belial eyed him intently, silently, waiting for him to continue his story.

"It started on Tuesday, I suppose," Cypress began. In reality, he had become curious earlier, but the day he spoke to Tony and heard about the scarves, the day he met Tai… that seemed like the best place to start.
"I spend a lot of time in the city. And you know as well as

I do that there's always somethin' going on, but I had a feeling this was somethin' different. So I started... well, this is going to sound creepy, and so much worse than it is..."

Belial's expression remained flat, listening passively to Cypress' spiel.

"I started following them. I followed them to Las Vegas."

"Followed who, exactly?" asked Belial, a smirk playing at the corner of his lips.

"Tai. Taina. The one with the scarves-"

The half-smile disappeared from Belial's face, his grip tightened on his glass and Cypress had the distinct feeling he'd said something very wrong.

"Mr. Rafferty," warned Belial in a low tone. "If you are to barge in here calling me King Belial, you shall afford the same courtesy to the rest of us. That includes King Paimon."

After a few seconds of looking upon Cypress' blank expression, Belial laughed. The sound was low and throaty, as if rustling through the foliage surrounding them.

His laughter subsided slowly, his eyes never leaving Cypress's face. To Cypress, it seemed as if Belial found endless entertainment in his bewilderment. In reality, though, the laughter stemmed more from relief - Cypress didn't know as much as Belial had feared.

There was also, on a deeper level, a touch of self-deprecating amusement in the demon king's mirth, reflecting on how worried he had been about this seemingly clueless man.

"*You didn't know!* You followed them all the way to another state, somehow figured me out along the way, but didn't manage to unveil them. They really are good at the whole secret thing," chuckled Belial.

His words brought highlighted excerpts from photocopied pages on the studio floor flooding back to Cypress' mind.

King Paimon.
King of the Djinni. Ruler of 200 legions. Known to appear as a strong woman or effeminate man wearing a golden crown. Believed to have great wisdom and the ability to reveal hidden truths…

Holy shit. Tai isn't a demonolator. They're a demon.

"I had no idea," whispered Cypress. "I swear, I thought they were a witch or something. Then I met Mr. Devas- King Asmodeus, I mean. I met King Asmodeus, and I worked out who he was-"

"That couldn't have been difficult," growled Belial with a subtle roll of his eyes. "He's barely even hiding in plain sight at this point, he's on full display, waving his giant… croc around."

"I mean, I only knew because I overheard Taina calling him by his name. I mean, Paimon! I'm sorry. This is all…

a lot," said Cypress, his voice wavering. "I overheard King Paimon calling him Asmodeus, and I didn't know what it meant. So I looked it up, and, well, here we are."

"You are an absolutely terrible storyteller, you know that?" sighed Belial. Cypress thought it best not to respond, simply nodding and looking into his empty glass as he felt his mouth grow dry. "Let's just get to what I *really* want to know, although I'm more confident that I'll like the answer after this revelation. How many of us have you unveiled?"

As he contemplated the names he'd highlighted and comparisons he'd drawn, Cypress' head began to spin, a nauseated feeling rising into his chest.

"Could I maybe have some more of that rum?" he managed to croak out. "I don't feel well."

"Sure," replied Belial, but he made no move to grab the bottle. Cypress watched him for a few seconds and eventually assumed that he was expected to pour his own drink. However, as he started to stand, he noticed that the small double-walled glass in his hand was already filled with spiced rum, a few tiny balls of ice floating in it.

"How—" gasped Cypress, trying hard not to drop the glass from his sweaty hand. He didn't finish his question. The man in front of him, according to the things he'd read, was one of the creators of the natural world. A ruler of the Underworld, ruling over eighty legions of lesser-ranked demons and fifty legions of spirits. A Fae King capable of unmatched levels of illusion and deception. And a trickster deity with the ability to shapeshift at will, which explained why every source's description of his visage was different.

Of course, he could pour rum without lifting a finger. He could probably turn the tide with the same ease.

The thought was terrifying, and Cypress took a deep gulp of his drink, hoping to swallow it down. The rum burned pleasantly as it went down, but did little to ease the knot of anxiety tightening in his chest. He glanced at Belial, who was watching him with a mixture of anticipation, mild amusement and something else - something far more ancient and inscrutable. The air in the room felt charged, as if even the plants around them were aware of the power dynamics at play. Cypress knew he was in over his head, but there was no turning back now.

"I figured out a few," he admitted. "You, of course. King Asmodeus. Duchess Crocell - at least I assume that's who the Secretary of State for Education, Eleanor Crouch is. And I saw Chantilly Charlemagne, the singer, milling around Tai's- King Paimon's- stall a few times, but I haven't worked out who she is yet. I know she must be one of you, though."

Belial chuckled. "What exactly makes you think she's one of us?"

"Well, that or she made a deal with y'all. But King Asmodeus owns half of Las Vegas, you control the media, Duchess Crocell influences the raising and education of the next generation - it's about power and influence, isn't it? And what greater power than to be adored by millions, having them sing your songs and dress like you?"

"I'm impressed," admitted Belial. "Yes, I suppose it is about power and influence, in a way. See, most deities, angels, demons, gods, you name it, they need you - people - *humans* - to survive.

Those, like me, who don't need it to survive, still rely on it to keep our power strong. People used to revere us and worship us, many moons ago, but outside of a tiny number of people who practice demonolatry and include us on their spiritual paths, we've largely been forgotten since we were demonized, our followers killed or forced to convert... so we're here, on this side of the veil. That's the only way to get interaction or energy these days."

Cypress stared at him in awe. "That... that actually makes a lot of sense, I guess," he shrugged, unsure what else to say. "So, just out of curiosity. Chantilly Charlemagne. She is one of you?"

"Yes, although if you've been looking at the entities who are traditionally considered female, I can't blame you for not getting that one. Have you come across the great Duke Amdusias in your research?"

"Yes!" proclaimed Cypress. "His musical instruments can be heard, but not seen. *That's why she never has a band on stage... of course.* But I read that he only gives concerts when commanded. Is that not true?"

Belial swirled his drink in his glass, looking pensively into it as if considering whether or not to answer.

"Well, I'd say that he - or rather she, Charlemagne - *is* being commanded. Her fans are always demanding more. More concerts, more albums, more personal details from a life they've no clue doesn't exist. And outside of that...

well, we're all under command, in a way."

Cypress wondered whether Belial might be deceiving him, the infamous Lord of Lies epithet hanging a question mark over every statement the demon made, but he had to know more.

"Under command from who?"

Belial looked up from his glass and into the other man's warm, trusting eyes. Cypress had often heard that the eyes were the windows to the soul, but up until this moment, he never understood what exactly that meant. Lost in the glacial depths of Belial's gaze, he felt naked and vulnerable, as if his soul was laid out on a yard sale table for all to peek and poke at.

"Now, you listen to me, *Kitty-Cat*," warned Belial, his voice lower now, raspier, huskier, more threatening. "I'm telling you this to satisfy your curiosity, so that you can live out the rest of your nine lives in peace. Not so that you can continue looking and endangering yourself and us. Is that clear?"

"Crystal," gulped Cypress, and not a second later, he felt his chair begin to shift under him.

He grasped the wooden arms of the chair, the Celtic-style carvings imprinting on his palm as his knuckles turned white, his heart pounding so hard against his ribcage that the echo whooshed and whirred in his ears. The chair moved slowly but deliberately, with an ominous dragging sound, towards Belial's desk, and when he finally dared to look down he found two thick vines, like monstrous versions of the braids of half-dry grass the girls back in Texas would craft bracelets out of in elementary school, wrapped around the legs of the chair, pulling him forward like the tentacles of a huge green octopus.

He resisted the urge to jump up, primarily because he was well aware that the vines would quickly switch to his legs over those of the chair if necessary, and quickly found himself inches from the face of Belial, who was leaning across his desk, his large hands clasped together.

Belial spoke quietly, measuring every word, clearly determined not to give too much away.

"Here's what I can tell you: when I say we're all following a command, I mean that we're acting on a plan made on the other side of the veil, by Emperor Lucifer."

"Like... Satan?" squeaked Cypress, digging his nails into his hand to stop himself descending into panic.

"Not at all. Satan simply means adversary, and is a title that's been ascribed to many... including myself. To my knowledge, the being I know as Lucifer is not one of them. A mistranslation at best, a smear campaign at worst - I digress. Not Satan. An ancient god of light, who has nobly earned his place at the top of our ranks. Most of us are directly following orders. In my case, well, he respects that I am, and forever will be, the One Without a Master, and I respect his wishes in return."

Cypress nodded, trying desperately to process what he was hearing.
Belial gave him no time to digest before continuing: "now,

not all seventy-two beings that you've read about are here. Not all of those who are on this side of the veil are in those texts. Not all of those you'd recognize are here in the USA. And here's the crucial part, Kitty: not all of the entities on this side of the veil are working in the interests of this planet or her people. That's why you need to leave this alone."

Staring defiantly into Belial's eyes, Cypress shook his head. "I can't just leave it. Especially not now."

Belial clenched his teeth, slamming a large fist down on the desk that shook the floor beneath Cypress.

"It's not optional," he snarled. "I told you what I could to ensure that your curiosity was quenched. You know who's who. You know who's behind it all. And you know why. Now you need to go back to your little easel, or whip up some peppermint punch cold foam for the same woman who's complained that it's too minty every single day for a month and orders it every single day anyway. That's your life, Mr. Rafferty. Not hunting down demons and playing Scooby Doo."

"Maybe I could help you," pleaded Cypress, but Belial's look silenced him instantly.

"You can help me by going home and forgetting this happened. Use it to inspire some art, think about it to make you feel more significant in this sickening, ruthless place. But stay out of it, do you hear me? I'd hate for you to have to disappear, but trust me, it's damn easy to make someone disappear in this city if necessary. *Stay. Out. Of. It.*"

A lump formed in Cypress' throat as he took in the threat,

and as the words looped in his head, he came to a nauseating realization. "The serial killer people are talking about," he gasped, feeling bile rising in his throat again. "That's you?"

Belial chortled heartily and shook his head derisively, openly mocking Cypress' naïveté. "You know, when you showed up outside, I really thought I'd be faced with someone far more intelligent. No, I'm not the serial killer, the Eat The Rich Killer, the boogeyman, whatever you want to call him. That's Bill."

"...Bill?"

"Yup. Figure that one out, Sherlock. But tell a soul - and trust me, I'll know - and I'll tell him you're on to us." Belial pushed an unassuming brown envelope across the desk towards Cypress. "It won't be pretty. And if you don't believe me, feel free to have a look in that envelope at what's left of the last few people who were considered a problem."

"I won't say anything to anyone," Cypress promised. "I swear to G… to Lucifer? Whoever I'm s'posed to swear to, I'll swear upon 'em ten times and hope to die."

"It might be wiser to hope not to," said Belial with a smile that somehow oozed equal parts charm and menace. "And I have no Gods or masters, so if you must swear upon a divine name in my presence, swear upon mine. Then I'll know you *really* mean it."

"Of course. I swear to you, King Belial…" Cypress clamored to find the words to say, every possibility feeling like a cliché from the fantasy films he'd watched as a teen. "I swear on Your Majesty and on your name that everything you've told me today and whatever I figure out from this point forward goes no further."

Belial nodded approvingly, then stood and walked to the door, not breaking eye contact with Cypress as it swung open a split before he laid a hand on the handle. Cypress jumped at the sight, wondering if he'd ever get used to these things, and played it off as standing up before walking to the door. As he reached it, Belial extended his hand once again, and Cypress accepted with less reluctance than when he'd arrived.

"It was a pleasure to meet you, Mr. Rafferty," said Belial - or rather, Bellisle. His voice had shifted to the pleasant, professional tone he used in television interviews, as if he'd flicked a switch.

"You too, Mr. Bellisle. I'm grateful for the information," Cypress replied, attempting to match the same tone, but betrayed by the slight tremble in his own voice.

"And I'm very grateful for your kind cooperation. Have a wonderful evening," nodded Bellisle. For a moment, Cypress almost wondered if he'd somehow imagined the past hour. The man before him seemed every inch the media tycoon the world knew him as; nothing about him even remotely resembled a demonic Fae king. But then, out of the corner of his eye, through the still half-open door behind Bellisle, he saw the chair he'd been sitting in being pulled back to its original spot by those grassy tendrils. *This was no figment of his imagination.*
With one more handshake and a forced smile, Cypress

nodded and turned towards the elevators. His feet carried him as if on autopilot, moving swiftly, with absolutely no intention of looking back.

As he walked, every surreal detail of the meeting swirled in his mind. The seemingly sentient greenery, the mysterious energy, and the unnerving hospitality of King Belial lingered, leaving Cypress' head flooded with disbelief and wonder.

Reaching the elevator, Cypress pressed the button and waited, the ding of the arriving cabin pulling him back to the present. As the doors slid open, he stepped inside, taking a deep breath to steady himself.

He knew that the world outside Bellisle's office would be just as it had been before - busy, noisy, but for the most part completely ordinary. And yet he couldn't shake the feeling that he was now part of a different world; a hidden one where that very same ordinary life was merely a thin veil over an extraordinary reality.

The early evening light cast long shadows on the skyscrapers, stretching across the crowded streets of New York City. This time, however, the shadows teemed with secrets, and the familiar lights seemed to pulse with new meaning.

Cypress walked with heightened awareness, each detail of his surroundings seemingly etched sharper than ever before. The everyday sights of the city had transformed, each one a stark reminder that even in the most familiar places, the unknown lurks just beneath the surface, waiting to be unearthed.

CHAPTER SEVEN

In the coming days, Cypress tried to carry on his daily life, stay out of it all as Belial had implored him. But there was one sentence the demon had uttered that refused to leave his mind: *"not all of those you'd recognize are here in the USA."*

He pinned the pages to the studio wall, connecting them with strings and colored pins, wondering constantly where in the world the rest of the demons he'd been researching were. *Could the King of England be King Baal? Maybe the ever-smiling French President, seemingly omnipresent on the television because of the upcoming elections, was Lucifer himself?*

And as he perused the possibilities, the rest of the world trundled on, largely unaware of the enigmatic forces pulling the strings, just out of sight.

Across the Atlantic Ocean, a certain silk-robed figure with beads in their ponytail had left Vegas behind, at least for now. They now charmed passers-by at a stall full of spectacular scarves in a buzzing cobblestone street in the heart of Brussels, biding their time until the shadowy hour of a late-night meeting with an old friend.

As the flow of people ebbed out and the stalls around them began to close for the evening, they slipped between the folds of fabric, disappearing from sight for a moment. Seconds later, they emerged wearing the same bespoke suit they'd worn to the casino. They smiled wryly at the double-takes from a few lingering stallholders, aware that behind the bewildered expressions, those people were undoubtedly doing extreme mental gymnastics to explain what they had just witnessed.

If only they could see this part, they thought to themself with a smirk, pulling the cover of the market stall closed just as everything inside dissipated into a wisp of pinkish smoke, reminiscent of a cloud at sunset, before disappearing completely. *Then they'd really lose their marbles.*

They walked briskly but with an effortless grace, flashing a smile to those who caught their eye and a wink to those whose gaze lingered, making their way towards the hotel their friend had chosen.

After a twenty-minute walk spent basking in the low sun and the attention of the locals, Paimon arrived at Hotel L'Amaryllis, a towering baroque edifice in the center of town, always exuding an air of pretentiousness. The hotel was a favored haunt of the European political elite - including, in this instance, socialist heavyweight Vincent van Leeuwenhoek.

Van Leeuwenhoek had been a household name across Europe for over a decade. As the man at the helm of the European freedom of movement project and an outspoken campaigner for regional unity, his presence in any setting was not unremarkable. Yet, as he waited in the grandiose lobby for Paimon, no one gave him a second glance.

Taller than most and built, as Andras once stated, "like a brick shithouse," Vincent's style made him no less conspicuous. He stood clad in mismatched tweed with brown leather shoes, waves of red hair cascading around his shoulders, and a short graying beard dusting his strong, square jawline. He would stick out anywhere, yet he had an uncanny ability to go unnoticed when he desired. An ability that, as it had many times before, was about to catch his old friend off guard.

Like clockwork, Paimon walked through the gilded glass doors of the hotel, and, as expected, right past Vincent, perching themself on a barstool not eight feet away. Vincent allowed them to order a drink before approaching them from behind and placing a large, paw-like hand firmly on their shoulder. "Well, well, well, *Taina*," he boomed. "Only ordering for one? I see how it is."

The djinn whipped their head around, coming face to face with the grinning, rosy-cheeked politician, and gave his shoulder a playful shove.

"I wish you wouldn't do that," they hissed. "I know it's useful for not being harassed when you're out and about, darling, but must you *really* play your games with me every time?"

Vincent's laugh thundered through the hotel bar, the sound bouncing off the walls as an elaborate pink and orange cocktail was placed in front of his companion. "What fun would it be if I didn't?"

Paimon rolled their eyes, then allowed their face to soften into a smile as the titanic redhead ordered himself a double whisky. *"Your finest, neat, in a warmed glass,"* they mouthed along with him, having heard the order so many times before.

When both were equipped with drinks, Paimon stood, gesturing for Vincent to lead the way. "Shall we?" they smiled, and the two made their way to one of the hotel's luxurious meeting rooms, reminiscing jovially about past meetings as they walked.

The meeting room was a true testament to the hotel's baroque splendor, and as the pair settled into the almost throne-like seats each side of an ornate wooden table older than the city itself, the atmosphere inside it changed, flipping in an instant like a coin in a game of chance.

"You know you're a good friend of mine, Vinnie, and I love you dearly," Paimon said quietly.

"But?" retorted Vincent, and Paimon nodded, wringing their hands nervously.

"But there are concerns. Not from me; from the other side of the veil."

"From Lucy?"
"Maybe if you didn't call him Lucy, he'd be less scrutinous

of your policies, dearie. You do yourself no favors. But, yes. The Emperor has expressed some… disquietude over a few of your policies and actions as of late."

Vincent took a swig of his whisky, looking between the plush pink velvet drapes out of the tall window, taking in the city lights outside.

"Which policies and actions seem to be an issue, Paimon?" he asked, annoyance becoming more obvious by the second in his voice.

"Don't shoot the messenger, Vine," sighed Paimon. Their friend raised an eyebrow at the sound of his true name, a silent acknowledgment that the masks were now fully off. Their appearances may have remained behind a smokescreen for the mere sake of convenience, but on every other level, all pretenses had been dropped. No longer were they Taina and Vincent, eccentric traveling salesperson and smooth-talking politician, meeting for a routine catch-up. They were King Paimon and Earl Vine, rulers of Hell and Djinni royalty, locked in a discussion that could alter the fate of their kind and the world itself.

The room seemed to dim, the mythological scenes painted on the ornate frescoes receding into the background as reality overshadowed them. The tension in the air thickened, as if the very atmosphere recognized the gravity of the moment. Paimon's voice, usually playful and light, now carried the weight of ancient authority.

"The stakes have never been higher," Paimon continued, their eyes meeting Vine's with resolve, but also apprehension. "Our decisions on this side of the veil will ripple through the fabric of reality itself. If those decisions are unwise, the consequences are catastrophic."

Vine leaned back, his once casual demeanor now replaced with the unmistakable stoic bearing of a millenia-old ruler. "Indeed," he replied. "But that doesn't answer my question. I am here to break down the walls that act as the pillars of conflict, are those walls not being broken? Countries being brought so close together that their nations are, for all intents and purposes, one. Which part of that is problematic in the eyes of our dear Emperor?"

"Are you breaking walls, dearie? Or are you constructing them?"

Paimon's question hung in the air, Vine considering the implications as they continued.

"Yes, certain countries are brought together, nations are mixing, walls are, at least at first glance, crumbling beautifully. But for those outside, the walls have never been higher. The name of this game was always equality. And now Emperor Lucifer demands reassurance that you are not, in place of bringing the destructive elites to an end, simply creating a slightly nicer one."

Vine laughed quietly, nodding as he took in the weight of Paimon's words.

"Well, I do see the thorn in this particular rose," he pondered. "Unfortunately, however, my influence is not limitless. I can only do what I can, where I can, and I can assure you and the Emperor that the walls within my reach are being brought to the ground. Look at it yourself. Less conflicts, more cooperation, that's what my goal has always been, and I do not appreciate the implication that my efforts thus far have been counterproductive."

Paimon took a long sip of their cocktail, the brightly colored, umbrella-adorned glass that had earlier matched their energy so well was suddenly in stark contrast with their stern demeanor. It now appeared to be a symbol of the duality within them; the ability to balance whimsy with gravity, mirth with might. The delicate paper umbrella twirled slowly between their fingers, a small distraction from the heavy thoughts swirling in their mind.

"There are also rumors that you're working with the Emperor's brother... with the Dark One. Do these rumors hold any truth?" they asked quietly.

"But of course," replied Vine with a smile, his forthright honesty on the matter taking Paimon by surprise. "Now is no time for petty games. You've said yourself that every move we make could tip the balance. Lord Lucifuge has the same end game as his brother, the Emperor, as well as you and me; to save humanity so that they can save us."

"No, no, *no*," wailed Paimon, each iteration of "no" accompanied by the sound of their delicate hand slamming against the wood of the table. "That's exactly the issue. Emperor Lucifer, myself, Belial, even Asmodeus deep down, regardless of what he says... we want to save them out of mercy and respect, not selfishness. Of course there's an aspect of self-preservation to it, but in no way is this a case of saving them so they can save us, as if they're just batteries on a life support machine. We are acting out of *love* for the civilization who have given us life, power, offerings and love since time immemorial, who have come to us for refuge and advice even when it could endanger them. Lucifuge Rofocale, on the other hand, would be happy with a captive supply as long as it kept his power and ego at full throttle. That's the difference between the Emperor and the Dark One."

Vine finished the remaining whisky in his glass and let out a sigh. "They don't love us, Paimon. Imagine this…"

He rose from his seat, and Paimon watched as his glamour dissolved slowly, his true appearance taking form before them. His red hair billowed out as it transformed into a true mane, framing an increasingly animalistic face.

Soon, he stood in the center of the room, towering over a still-seated Paimon at nine feet tall, a gargantuan man with the head of a lion dressed in the striking red, teal and gold regalia of a Cossack soldier.

He let out a snarling roar, close enough to Paimon for his hot breath to swirl around their face.

"Imagine if I walked out of this room like this, out into the street. Would they love me?"

"They'd be scared, that's all," pleaded Paimon, but Vine chuckled darkly in response.

"And what do they do with things they're scared of?" he rumbled. "They try to assert their dominance over them. They torture, rape and kill them. Take them to labs and do experiments, cutting them up alive to try to understand them so that they might not be so scared any more. So I ask again: if I were to walk out there, or show up in the European Parliament like this-" he ran a rugged, hairy baseball glove-sized hand through his mane to accentuate his point - *"would they love me?"*

"I never said they would," sighed Paimon wearily. "That'll be a learning curve for them, and it's not going to happen overnight. But simply because many of them would show us no mercy or love, it doesn't mean we can't show it to them. We are far older and wiser, unmarred by religion and prejudice."

Vine snorted, gradually shifting back into his human glamour. "You've gone soft, old friend. Now, listen: I have no intention of working against you, but I do stand with Lord Lucifuge on this. I'll help to save them because we *need* them, not because I like them."

Huffing in frustration, Paimon decided against antagonizing the other djinn any further, instead reaching into his leather notebook case and pulling out a poster.

"You know who also stands with the Dark One, and is far more of a problem right now?" they asked, pushing the poster across the desk to Vine.

"Goran Labaš?" he asked warily, looking down at an election poster written entirely in Croatian. "He's a Presidential candidate in Croatia. By all accounts, the lad is mad as a March hare, but I highly doubt that he's any real threat to Emperor Lucifer, whether or not he's a follower of Lucifuge."

"Have you met him?" inquired Paimon, in a tone that made

the hair on Vine's arms prickle. The question was clearly loaded.

"I haven't," he admitted. "I've met the incumbent, but Labaš is a controversial figure to say the least, so I've been in no hurry to make his acquaintance."

"I think it's time to start being in a hurry, dearie," said Paimon. "Maybe then you'd recognize him. And if you're close to the Dark One, you could be our only hope of putting a stop to whatever it is he thinks he's going to do."

Vine grabbed the poster, looking at it closer, scanning the text for clues as to the true identity of the pale, dark-eyed, pointy-faced figure smirking back at him. Paimon placed a hand on the poster, and as they did, the paper began to ripple like water, the mysterious candidate's image now resembling a reflection in a deep purple lake. Slowly, the image of the young man contorted, his long, angular nose lengthening even further, the whites of his nearly-black eyes disappearing. But before the true image, a statuesque off-white borzoi dog with magnificent black feathered wings, could fully appear, something else caught Vine's eye. At Paimon's touch, the name on the poster had changed too.

Vine slapped Paimon's hand away from the poster, swearing loudly, and jumped to his feet.

"Why? How was this allowed to happen?!"

Paimon shrugged, unable to answer as they were drinking the remaining half of their cocktail in one long gulp. When they were finished, they stood too, facing Vine from the other side of the table.

"I don't know, sweetheart, I suggest you ask good ol' Lucifuge about that. What I do know is that Glasya-Labolas is chaos incarnate, and he was supposed to be here to help dismantle old structures of power where needed. If he becomes part of it... I can only imagine the mayhem and violence that would ensue."

Vine nodded in agreement, sending a wave of relief flooding through Paimon's body.

"As I said, I'm fully on board with the plan, as is Lord Lucifuge. Our motives may differ, but we have far more in common than that which divides us, and to allow this would be a monumental mistake. I will cross the veil tonight and put this to Lord Lucifuge, and we'll ensure that Goran decides to retire from politics and move to Costa Rica - in other words, that Glasya is exiled firmly back to the other side."

"Thank you, Vine," breathed Paimon, pulling his friend into an embrace. "I knew I could count on you."

"You never have to doubt that," said Vine softly, patting Paimon's back before stepping back to look them in the eye. "I will always do whatever it takes to help you, or any one of our own. I can only hope that you soon find your own priorities in the same place."

CHAPTER EIGHT

Back in New York City, in a twenty-ninth floor apartment overlooking a street filled with cheap bodegas, dive bars and a tattoo parlor frequented by bikers and ex-cons, Cypress Rafferty stared at his smartphone, debating with himself in his head over what to do next.

Dozens of calls from his girlfriend, Mialani, had gone unanswered, numerous texts replied to with a vague **"Sorry, mega busy"** or **"We'll talk about it soon"**, and now, unsurprisingly, he found himself looking down at a long message where she made her feelings on his behavior abundantly clear.

Hey. I don't know what's up with u but I haven't seen u in like 2 weeks. If u aint happy then u should have the balls to tell me that, and if it's nothing I did then I deserve better than this. I'm coming over after work (my shift finishes at 10 now, which u might know if u ever cared to ask) and I aint leaving til you open the door and talk to me. Shutting me out like this is not ok Cy. See you soon. Lani

"Dang it," he muttered, glancing at the time in the corner of the screen. 10:34; Mialani would be arriving at any second. He looked around the room, fraught with nerves, unsure whether he should pull down all of his research and investigation and make up a story, or whether he should go against Belial's warnings and tell her the truth, risking both of their lives at the hands of Bill - whoever he may be.

His panicked pacing was interrupted by the intercom phone buzzing loudly, indicating his girlfriend's arrival. He gritted his teeth and pressed the button to let her in, knowing that, even with the short walk to the elevators and the trip to the second-highest floor, he had under two minutes until an irate woman stood in the doorway demanding answers.

A minute and fifty seconds later, though he'd never admit he was counting, a sharp knock on his apartment door told him that she had arrived.

Opening the door just far enough for them to look at each other, he blurted out the first thing he could think of that might make her turn on her heel and leave.

"It's someone else," he stated, his stomach twisting into a painful knot at the thought of wounding her with such a hurtful lie.

The four months they'd spent together, while brief, had taught him both peace and wild the likes of which he'd never known, and he hated that he was ending it in this way, but in his mind, the truth was not an option. "I've been cheating on you. I'm sorry, Lani."

To Cypress' surprise, Mialani didn't cry, scream or run, or even, as he'd momentarily feared, take a swing at him. She... laughed. She shook her head and let out a short peal of laughter, making him pause and wonder what was coming next.

"The hell you have," she snorted. "I can tell when you're lying from a mile off, boy, now get out of my way."

She pushed past Cypress, sweeping into his apartment in a gust of cocoa butter-scented air, but stopped dead in her tracks when she saw the wall covered with book pages, hand-scrawled notes and strings.

"Is this why you ain't been around? A goddamn *art project?*" she snapped. She snatched the black baseball cap from her head and threw it down on the desk next to Cypress' laptop before walking over to the wall, examining the disorderly display on it. He watched her every move. How her feet shifted, the rubber sole of her plimsolls scraping against the floorboards. How her hands moved from the pockets of her denim Bermuda shorts to trace strings between papers and back to her pockets again. He just stood, and watched, waiting for her to speak.

When she finally did, her voice was quiet. "This ain't no regular art project, is it, Cy? What the hell is all of this?"

She spun to face him, confusion and concern in her deep brown eyes.

"I can't tell you, baby," he choked, to which Mialani threw her hands in the air.

"That's always it with you, isn't it, Cypress? You don't know how to communicate. You ignore me for two weeks for some stupid project, and now what? Your precious creative process is more important than me understanding why? I'm done. I'm *so* done."

She grabbed her cap from the desk and started towards the door, but Cypress called her name and against her better judgment, she stopped.

"I'll tell you everything," he promised, the words out of his mouth before he could stop them. "Please just let me explain."

Mialani let out an exasperated grunt, but, in no small part due to her own need for answers, she turned back to face him. "Fine. But this better be good, and you best make it quick too."

He sat down on the same olive-green faux leather sofa he'd slept on the first night Mialani stayed over after a few too many beers, where she'd perched excitedly watching him watch her favorite movie for the first time, where she'd attempted to lay for him to paint her before discovering that she couldn't stop laughing for long enough to assume a sultry pose. The memories hung in the air as he gestured for her to join him, but she seemed nonplussed, focused only on the promised explanation.

"Well?" she prodded, and Cypress placed a hand on her arm, unsure whether it was for his own comfort or hers, and began to talk.

He lost track of time as he talked, barely drawing breath as he recounted every detail in hushed tones, reminding Mialani at the end of every other sentence that their very lives, and possibly the whole world, were in grave danger should she say a peep to anyone.

When he was finished, he took a deep, shaky breath and looked at his girlfriend, who was shaking her head in disbelief. "I can't believe it," she breathed.

"I know, it's a lot to take in-" Cypress began, but she interrupted, jumping to her feet.

"No, asshole. I can't believe *you*. You treat me like this, you pretend that you're cheating on me, then you sit me down to supposedly tell me the truth, only to make even more of a mockery out of me? That is so messed up. I'm leaving."

"Lani, please," he called, but it fell on deaf ears.

"Forget it," she told him from the doorway, a solemn sadness in her face and voice. "You're either drunk, high or a straight-up douchebag. And I ain't got time for any of those things. Goodbye, Cypress."

The door slammed behind her and Cypress sunk back onto the sofa, unable to stop tears from flooding down his cheeks. Emotions mixed and tangled in his chest like the strings on the wall, regret taking center stage. Regret for not including Lani from the start, or maybe for telling her at all. Regret for bothering Bellisle and getting in so far over his head. Regret for even asking Tony about the weird person across the road and their stupid scarves.

The days after she left blurred into one. Day became night and night became day as Cypress became consumed with the need to find out more, to know everything about the world that was pulling his life from under his feet, and to somehow prove it to Mialani.

His studio, once dotted with half-finished canvases, was now littered with empty pizza boxes, takeout cartons and energy drink cans, a grim expression of his decline into despair and desperation. The papers and strings took over another wall, then a third, before the sound of the intercom phone pulled him back to the real world.

He ran to the handset, picking it up with one hand and crossing his fingers with the other. "Lani?"

"No," replied the crackly voice on the other side. "It's Noah. You need to let me in, dude."

Cypress groaned, leaning against the wall next to the intercom, and pressed the button. Noah Taylor, an abstract artist whose shock of auburn hair and countless tattoos were a familiar sight at the city's art fairs, had quickly become Cypress' first friend in New York. Over the years, their bond had only deepened, and if there was any chance of anyone believing the madness that Cypress's life had become and helping him navigate it, it would be Noah. Despite that, though, Cypress knew that the story wouldn't be an easy sell, and his hope diminished further when he opened the door to find Noah not alone but standing with three other people.
To Noah's right stood Ulysses Broussard, a short, stout African American man whose twin sister Apollonia was a close friend of Mialani. The four of them had spent

countless evenings laughing over drinks and snacks or watching football games that only Ulysses was truly invested in, while the rest drank in his contagious enthusiasm. But now, his jovial demeanor was nowhere to be seen, replaced by a quiet unease.

To his left, staring at Cypress with similar apprehension, were the two women who shared his shift at Pressed. The younger and shorter of the two was Zip—short for Zipporah, a name only her mother was allowed to use—a petite befreckled red-haired party animal in her early twenties. Beside her stood Kaia, a philosophy graduate with a dry sense of humor, an entirely black wardrobe, and a seemingly limitless supply of eyeliner. The two were the epitome of "opposites attract" and often joked that Cypress was the balance between them—not as glittery and lively as Zip but far less quiet and brooding than Kaia. The three had become firm friends at work, and seeing the women here felt like smelling salts under Cypress's nose, a stark reminder of life outside the studio.

"What is this?" Cypress asked cautiously, addressing his question directly to Noah.

Noah attempted a smile, but managed an uncomfortable grimace, while Ulysses answered for him. "It's an intervention, man. Lani told Apollonia at their queer women of color brunch thing that you two broke up, said something about how you were drunk and lying. I didn't think that sounded like you, so I managed to find Noah online and asked him if he'd heard from you, he said no. So we met up and went to your job to talk to you, and what did we find? These chicks saying you called in to quit with no warning and won't answer their calls."

Cypress opened his mouth to respond, but the other man continued.

"At that point we start thinkin' you might have died or some shit. So I got Lani's number from my sister and asked her to meet me and Noah to talk. She told us everything, man, but it don't sound like you to make all of that up just to mess with her, so that means you're... you know. There's something not right with your mind or whatever."

"He's saying that we're worried about your mental health, Cy," Zip chimed in, her somber tone a million miles from her usual gleeful giggles and musical outbursts. "We just want to come in and talk."

"The place is kinda messy," reasoned Cypress, "I appreciate it and all but I'm good. Maybe y'all can come back another time?"

"I don't care about a little mess," Noah told him. "We need to talk. Please let us in."

Cypress stepped aside and let the group enter, hearing their whispers as they did.

"I told you it was kinda-"

"This isn't kinda messy, Cy. This is a biohazard," Kaia told him bluntly. "I'm gonna start cleaning while you talk to them, you can't live like this. Where are the trash bags?"

He pointed to the cupboard under the sink, unable to meet her eye, as Zip pushed a can out of the way with a sequinned combat boot. "Let's all help with cleaning," Zip suggested, picking the can off the floor and placing it into the bag her coworker just opened. "We can talk while we clean."

And so the five got to work as Cypress recounted the same story he'd told Mialani, adding in the conclusions he'd come to in the anguished days of research since.

"It's Andras," he whispered, pointing to a photocopied image of an owl-headed man riding a wolf, holding a sword in the air. "That's Bill!"

Ulysses studied the image quietly for a few seconds before reading the information below it aloud.

"As one of Hell's most notorious entities, Andras holds the title of a great Marquis, commanding thirty legions of demons. He is often depicted as a warrior with the body of an angel and the head of an owl or raven, riding a fearsome black wolf.

Known for his ruthless nature, Andras has a fearsome reputation for causing death and destruction. He is particularly infamous for his inclination to kill or harm humans, often turning those who summon him against their enemies or even against themselves. He is driven by an insatiable desire for violence and bloodshed…"

Cypress nodded frantically, pointing at Ulysses, urging the others to listen.

"You see? Head of an owl or raven! He has a beak - a *BILL* - and he's known to enjoy killing people! It's him!"

"You're telling me this thing is real, it's the Eat The Rich Killer, and it's coming after you?" Ulysses asked, the doubt dripping from his voice.

"Well, hopefully he's not coming after me yet. I don't think he knows I told Lani, or I'd already be dead. And if he doesn't know I told her, then he won't know I told you. So we're safe."

"Oh, I am *so* glad that I'm safe from a stabby bird riding a wolf," Zip mocked, stopping when Kaia gave her a sharp dig in the ribs. "Sorry, Cy. It's just… this is insane. You see that, right?"

Noah nodded in agreement, placing a hand on Cypress' shoulder with a weak smile full of pity. "You need to let this stuff go, dude. I've seen the person with the scarves, they're just a weirdo. A weirdo who clearly has a talent for sleight of hand, but come on, you can't lose your mind over some charlatan with magic tricks and sketchy friends."

"I was in Belial's office, Noah," insisted Cypress, tears pooling in his eyes. "You gotta believe me, he filled my glass up without touching a thing, and those vine things…"

"They were pulling the chair around, you told us," nodded Kaia. "Look, we're not saying you're making this up. We're saying that you need to get help."

She shot a glance to Ulysses, who pointed a chubby finger at Cypress, smiling. "You know, this just means you're a great artist, man!" he declared with a grin he hoped looked more real than it felt. "Your guy Van Gogh was a little bit cuckoo, and Dali too! All the best artists are!"

"Not helpful," hissed Zip, and Cypress swatted Noah's hand from his arm, storming over to one of the walls covered in the fruits of his research.

"I'm not *crazy*," he insisted, his voice raising in volume and pitch with every word. He started grabbing handfuls of paper and string, pulling his demented tapestry down from the wall, throwing ripped pieces and loose pins to the floor.

Noah and Kaia followed him as he went, exchanging fearful looks as they pushed the remnants of his rage into trash bags until all three walls were bare.

"Do y'all feel better now?" he shouted, kicking the closest bag over. "Are you happy, now that you've come in here, called me crazy and taken all of this away from me for your own comfort?"

"We're trying to help you, Cy," said Zip softly, but he responded with a derisive laugh.

"Helping me figure this crap out, helping me deal with it, hearing me out and helping me convince Lani that I'm not a weapons-grade asshole, that would be helping. Inviting yourselves into my apartment, judging me and refusing to even consider that what I'm saying might be true? If that's helping, who needs hindrance?"

"That's not fair, man," warned Ulysses. "This girl just swept your floor and changed your sheets out of her own goodwill so that you don't have to live in a damn dumpster. The least you could do is show her some respect."

"It's okay," sighed Zip. "I know he didn't mean it like that. Let's just go."

Cypress stared out of the window, refusing to look at any of his friends as they gathered up overfilled trash bags and silently exited the apartment, softly closing the door on him both literally and figuratively as they left. He continued to watch as they emerged from the door below, looking like tiny video game versions of themselves. They crossed the road towards a dumpster tucked in an alleyway between two bars, talking urgently as they went.

As they loaded bag after bag into the dumpster in the dim, flickering light of a nearby streetlight, Kaia was the first to utter the unspeakable. "What if he's right?"

"Not you too," groaned Ulysses. "I ain't saying demons and spirits ain't real, shit, my mom is from New Orleans. I know about voodoo and hoodoo and things that go bump in the dark better than you do, I can tell you that much. But these things on these pages? Disguised as people, trying to save the world, and somehow he's the chosen one who gets to see it all? Come on now."

Kaia gave an insincere smile of acknowledgement, but then Zip spoke, her voice hoarse. "What if some of it is real, but he got it wrong?"

"What do you mean?" asked Kaia, her heart rate rising rapidly.

"Alright, I'm out," barked Noah, throwing his last bag into the dumpster. "I'll get the subway home, I'm not listening to any more of this."

He turned and walked away, but other than a halfhearted "hey, man…" from Ulysses, there was no attempt to stop him; the others were now listening intently to Zip.

"Well, he said that a lot of the demons are influential or powerful, right? So what if he was onto something with the Eat The Rich Killer stuff, but he's a demon hunter, and the *victims* were the demons?"

Her words hung in the air, the other two weighing up the implications and what to say next.

"There's only one way to find out for sure," reasoned Kaia. "We gotta pull those papers back out of the bags."

The same second, before anyone had a chance to reach for a bag or even draw breath, a figure lurched from behind the dumpster, a black hoodie shrouding his face. Homeless people behind dumpsters are no rarity in a city like New York, but as this one emerged from the shadows, the dim light illuminated the metallic glint of a blade in his gloved hand.

"He's got a knife," Zip screamed, already sprinting towards the street, closely tailed by Kaia.

"Hey, fuck you, drunk-ass bum," hollered Ulysses at the menace charging towards them, but, unarmed and increasingly alarmed by the speed the figure was gaining, he quickly turned and fled too.

Only once in the relative safety of the street, in the clear view of cars, bars and windows, did they stop and look back, but there was no sign of their pursuer. Unwilling to give him a chance to reappear, they ran to the parking lot behind Cypress' apartment block and piled into Zip's sky blue Beetle, sweaty, shaken but headed for safety.

With them gone, a dark hooded figure in a nearby alleyway tucked away his Swiss army knife and threw a lit match into a loaded dumpster. And when the flames had spread enough to ensure the contents would never see the light of day again, a large, majestic barn owl rose with the smoke and flew into the night sky.

CHAPTER NINE

As night once more turned to morning over America's most densely-populated city, one of its myriad of inhabitants tossed and turned in the first set of clean bedsheets that had graced his bed in weeks.

Outside, the city he'd come to call his home no longer beckoned lovingly. It seemed that the constant roar of traffic and music were there purely to drown out the whispers in the shadows, the ever-present bright lights serving only to blind the rest of the world from the truth.

And in an office filled with plants, on the forty-ninth floor of one of the city's tallest skyscrapers, a pink-haired girl dressed entirely in matching blush tones was as blind as blind could be.

"I checked with the technicians, they said the studio is all ready for the interview, the cameras are set up and the journalist - Anastasia, is it? - she's in the backroom already, going over her notes with Enric."

"Going over her notes, is that what they're calling it?" smirked Matt Bellisle, earning a quizzical look from his intern, who was quite obviously unable to work out what else their most senior journalist would be doing with the junior news editor.

"How do I put this in a kid-friendly way?" he perused, ignoring her usual theatrical pout at being referred to as a kid. "They're *sitting in a tree, K-I-S-S-I-N-G.* Everyone knows they have a good thing going, I don't give a damn and nor should you. I can only hope she had the sense to *actually* go over her notes first so she doesn't screw this up. This is the biggest interview of this year, I need it to go well."

"Oh! Oh, I didn't... wow! Okay," giggled Camilla. "Just as well I didn't go in to check on her, then." She cleared her throat and looked at the floor, trying not to let the room fall into an awkward silence. "I'm sure she did. She's very competent, she knows what she's doing."

Bellisle let out a loud *"Ha!"* and approached the intern, smiling softly. "I have more experience with people than your imagination could ever comprehend," he told her, knowing that she was oblivious to the depth of the truth in his statement. "If there's one piece of advice I can give you, it's this: never assume that people know what they're doing, much less that they'll do the right thing if their own selfish interests are involved."

Before Camilla could respond, the door creaked open slightly before swinging wide, revealing a slim yet curvy woman with a bouncy blonde blow-dry, dressed in a figure-hugging royal blue skirt suit and matching patent heels.

"Bill told me I could come right on up," she explained to Bellisle before turning her attention to Camilla. "I'm sorry, how rude of me," she said, her voice reminiscent of windchimes and warmth radiating from her smile. "We haven't met. I'm Eleanor Crouch."

"I know," grinned Camilla, before realizing that her comment may have struck the Secretary of State as rude and scrambling to explain. "I didn't mean- I just meant that I recognized you! It's nice to meet you. I'm Camilla. Camilla Jenkins, I'm an intern here, I work for Mr. Bellisle."

"Well, it is a pleasure to meet you too, sweet girl," laughed Crouch, pulling the floundering teenager in for a fleeting hug. "Tell me, is Mr. Bellisle kind to you?"

Camilla nodded eagerly, looking over the older woman's shoulder at her boss. "He's the best," she said, and Crouch let out another melodic titter.

"And how much does he pay you to say that?" she teased, with Bellisle grinning mischievously behind her.

"Now, now, Ellie. You're not the only one who knows how to make friends and influence people. I'll have you know she's paid more than generously, but that's irrelevant to the fact that I *am* the best."

"Your ego knows no bounds, Matanbuchas Bellisle. Sweet Camilla, would you mind giving us a few minutes alone? I have some points I need to discuss with the boss man here before my interview."

Camilla quickly excused herself, gingerly closing the door behind her, and Crouch turned to face Bellisle. "She doesn't know who you are, does she? We can't let them get too close, you know that," the blonde said quietly.

"She doesn't," Bellisle assured her, choosing to ignore the second half of her words lest he reveal a far more disconcerting truth. "Judging by the golden retriever head tilt when you said my full first name, I don't think she even knew that. As far as she's concerned, I'm just the guy she learns about at college, with a lot of money and a lot of time and advice for her, and she appreciates that. And I appreciate having someone who's not Andras in my office occasionally. There's less chance of the snacks she brings me having thumb tacks in them, for one thing."

"I'm not even going to ask about Andras," Crouch tutted. "I suppose it's nice to see that even on this side of the veil, with different faces and names and jobs, the dynamic between you two hasn't changed."

"The more things change, the more they stay the same," shrugged Bellisle. "Even you, Crocell. Your voice can still charm the birds out of the trees. That's why this interview is so important - trust in politicians is at an all-time low, and you can't blame 'em. Unfortunately, that includes you, so now we have to set you apart from the rest. Use your voice, your siren song, and tell them what they want to hear."

"I know what I'm doing, Belial," she told him, her chocolate-brown eyes darkening with resentment. "My issues are two: firstly, I understand that you've chosen to give me a human journalist. This could have been staged far better had we used one of your legionnaires, they're swarming the place anyway. Even Andras would have made more sense."

"Andras is the ink-and-paper kind of journalist - at least his minions are, and he puts his name in the byline. He doesn't do TV work. I assure you that Anastasia Tsakonas is the best person for this job, not least because the people out there absolutely love her. Do you know how many clips of her interviews have gone viral? Think what that would do for us - your voice, your charm, on millions of screens worldwide."

"I do hope you're right," Crocell sighed, smoothing her skirt. "Let's do this, then."

Minutes later, she was on air, expertly weaving a passionate vision. Her voice, soft and smooth, painted a world where education was a realm of limitless possibilities. She spoke of a system that offered every American the best start in life, from their first day of kindergarten to their PhD graduation,

Across the country, viewers were captivated by her words, carefully crafted to transcend political divides. Enchanted seemingly by her eloquence, people from all walks of life found themselves united, if only for a moment, by the power of her vision.

With one exception, that is.

Sixteen blocks away, Cypress sat up in bed, still wrapped in his slightly worn turquoise-colored blanket, and reached for the remote, turning on the television on the wall opposite him. The screen buzzed to life, revealing a polished news studio.

The camera was zoomed in on a smiling blonde woman, her voice smooth and captivating, as she spoke about a visionary education system. While the rest of the world nodded along approvingly, Cypress felt a chill run down his spine. It was her. The one who started it all. Duchess Crocell, the one who'd tipped his curiosity over the edge at Taina's - *King Paimon's* - stall. Her words shimmered as brightly to Cypress as they did to everyone else, but he knew they were a masterful blend of sincerity and manipulation, designed to ensnare hearts and minds.

Fury surged through him, and without thinking, he hurled the remote control at the screen. The device struck the television with a dull thud, falling to the floor with no effect on the picture.

Cypress' mind raced as the demoness continued talking. The bespectacled interviewer, sitting across from her with a placid smile, caught his attention. He'd seen her many times before, but now, she presented a new mystery. Was she in on it? Was she one of them? Or just another unsuspecting human, charmed by their facade? The doubt gnawed at him, the relentless questioning of who was a demon and who wasn't, and if they were, which one they were.

He rubbed his temples, trying to push the thoughts away. He hated that the knowledge that demons walked among ordinary people, some in positions of power and influence, was a burden he carried alone. There were no others to share the weight, no allies. Just him, isolated and overwhelmed, struggling to navigate a world where the lines between good and evil, human and spirit, blurred beyond recognition.

He found himself wondering for what seemed like the millionth time where the other demons were, what they were doing. Were they all playing some twisted game, manipulating humans from the shadows for their own sick entertainment? Or was Belial telling the truth; were some of them genuinely trying to help, to fulfill their original purpose? The uncertainty was maddening.

He stood up and crossed the room to retrieve the remote from where it had landed. His fingers tightened around it, knuckles whitening as he pressed the red button with perhaps a bit too much force, and when the image flickered to black and hum of the cars on the street below replaced the dulcet tones of Crocell, he took a deep breath of relief.

Seeing a beam of sunlight flooding through the window onto the floor, he let his blanket drop from around his waist, walking nude into the warm glow. He sat on the floor, allowing it to wash over him, and closed his eyes.

Beyond the veil, Emperor Lucifer looked on sadly. It had brought the Lightbringer untold joy for more years than one could count to see the creatures on the other side basking in the radiance of his energy, but this one was different. Sad. Lost.

Cypress ran his fingers through his hair, bathing in the light. *Is this what it feels like to be baptized?*

The light seemed to caress him, sweeping away the exhaustion and oppression that had become his new normal. *I wonder if anyone ever drowned during their baptism.*

The thought crashed over his head like a cymbal, echoing through his mind with an intensity that left him momentarily disoriented. He scrambled to his feet, his heart pounding in his chest, and staggered backward, away from the warm embrace of the sunray. When he looked back at the floor, breathing hard as if he truly had just been pulled from the depths of the sea, the beam of light had retreated too. It was no longer flooding across the floorboards but hanging outside the window like a shimmering mist, streaming from between the two tired, dingy buildings opposite, pulling back towards them slowly like a calm tide.

He watched for a few seconds before exhaling slowly, grasping at his hair in frustration. *It was just the sun. Can't I even trust the sun?*

Unbeknownst to him, there was a reason for his unease, and in his lush verdant office nearby, Matt Bellisle groaned as the same golden beam of light poured through his window, cascading between leaves and vines. Within seconds, a man emerged from the glow dressed in pristine white robes adorned with intricate gold embroidery, moving slowly with an ethereal grace. His thick, wavy light brown hair fell around his jawline, catching the light to transform into a halo of spun gold that framed his features. His deep golden brown eyes, like pools of molten amber, were already locked on Bellisle, radiating ancient wisdom and unspoken power, and more pertinently, a menacingly quiet wrath.

"Emperor Lucifer," smiled Bellisle, holding out a hand.

"To what do I owe the honor?"

The Lightbringer declined the handshake with a curt shake of the head, taking a step closer to the taller man.

"King Belial, a scorpion in my bed sheets as ever," he drawled, his soft voice sharpened by anger. "Did you not think to tell me that you spoke my name and unveiled us all to a human?"

"The human figured it out on his own," insisted Belial, but his words went unheeded.

"You are, are you not, the Lord of Lies?" hissed Lucifer. "Would it be so unthinkable to convince the man he was imagining the whole thing, then tell Asmodeus to tighten up his mask before it falls off altogether? The one time you decide to value the truth, *Your Majesty*, is the one time it could easily cost us everything."

His mocking tone on Belial's title stung, but the demon refused to stand down.

"You know that's not true. The title of Lord of Lies is just as much about uncovering truths as concealing them."

"I am not an imbecile, Belial, though it appears you are. This is one truth you should have concealed at all costs, do you understand that?" barked Lucifer, and Belial instinctively took a step back. In years reaching innumerability, the occasions on which the Emperor lost his temper could be counted on one hand, but when it happened it rarely ended well.

Belial's mind was yanked back to an incident in days long gone, etched in the annals of infernal history. One member of his own vast legions, a boisterous lower-ranking demon named Bilanoch, had made the fateful decision to challenge the authority of Emperor Lucifer. In a brazen and ill-fated gambit, Bilanoch sought to orchestrate a coup. He gathered a cadre of rebels under the shroud of night and conceived a plan to abduct the Emperor's consort, Empress Lilith, as she tended her beloved black apple orchard, using her as bait to lure the Lightbringer to his eternal darkness.

But fate, ever the arbiter of justice, had a different design.

One of the rebels, driven perhaps by a flicker of loyalty or simply self-preservation, betrayed the plot to the Emperor. That day, and that day only, Belial witnessed the unbridled fury in Lucifer's eyes—the same searing, incandescent rage he beheld now.

The memory continued to unfurl with an unwelcome vivid clarity; Bilanoch was stripped and bound by the Empress' handmaidens to a floating wheel known as Icarus' Sundial, a sadistic device crafted as a coronation gift by the most bloodthirsty of Andras' legions. To Belial's knowledge, it had never been used until that day, nor had it been since.

The wheel was cursed to follow the relentless path of the sun, rotating and adjusting its position to ensure the condemned was perpetually bathed in its blistering heat. There was no respite, no shadowed reprieve from the agony.

As the sun completed its inexorable journey across the sky, the wheel along with it, Belial had looked upon the charred, blistered husk that was once his soldier. The sight was a grim testament to the fact that light, as well as being the catalyst of life and growth, was no less capable of destruction, and now, as the same flames of fury flickered in the Lightbringer's eyes, he struggled to mask his trepidation.

"I wouldn't be able to tie you to the Sundial if I wanted to, Belial, and I am not a cruel enough man to do so," said Lucifer, doubtless having seen the memories flashing through the demon's eyes. "Had that wretched rat not boasted to his co-conspirators about the ways in which he intended to violate my wife after capturing her, I would have been far more merciful with his death. You know that. But do you know who *would* tie you down and torture you for being too loud about this?"

He raised a hand, pointing out of the window towards the streets below.

"King Paimon came to me after a conversation with Earl Vine recently. They were most perturbed that my dear brother and Vine resent the humans, believing that if they knew the truth they'd conduct terrible experiments as they do with the wonderful creatures of the animal kingdom. I told them the same thing I'll tell you now. The only difference between me and my brother is that I believe humans are worthy of forgiveness, and of love, regardless of that. I've no doubt that it would be the case."

Belial stayed silent, allowing the Emperor to continue, but before he could, they were distracted by the rattle of the handle of the office door. "Yes?" called Belial, and he was answered by a familiar brash, raspy voice.

"It's Bill. Open the damn door, Bel!"

Before Belial could open his mouth to remind Lucifer who Bill was, his colleague appeared, pulled through the door seemingly by an invisible hand, as if the wooden panel was made of softened butter. "What the fu-" he squawked, stopping himself when he laid eyes on the vision in white in front of him.

"Emperor Lucifer! I wasn't expecting you, Your Grace," he said, shaking himself off and smoothing down his shirt.

"Lord Andras," smiled the Emperor, his voice still laced with commination. "Were you aware of Belial's... lapse in judgment?"

"With the chick from the diner? I don't think he knew she was married," he crowed, and Lucifer landed a warning slap on the side of his head in response.

"I have neither the time nor the will to listen to idiocy," he snapped. "Are you, or are you not, aware of the problem named Cypress Rafferty?"

Knowing better than to crack another joke, Andras responded with a quiet *"I am."*

"I was summoned, for want of a better word, last night," he continued. "He had some papers, and on one of them was my sigil with some information. One of his friends was reading it out, and you know that when someone is touching the sigil and saying your name, you kinda get... dialed in."

Emperor Lucifer stood straight upright, only having focused on one part of his explanation.

"Does this mean that there are others who know?"

Andras shook his head fervently, having heard from the shadows the conversations within Cypress' apartment. "He tried to tell them. They didn't listen, they thought he was bat-tits insane and took out all of the papers into the trash. The two chicks started sounding like they might wanna check everything out to be sure, so I chased 'em and set fire to the lot. The paper, not the chicks."

"I am deeply concerned that such a clarification was needed at the end of that sentence, Andras, but thank you for handling it uncharacteristically sensibly," acknowledged Lucifer before turning back to Belial. "You, on the other hand, have handled this abysmally, and I implore you to fix it before it's too late."

"Any attempt to contact Mr. Rafferty again could make things worse," warned Belial, but the Emperor was unwilling to accept any excuses.

"Then find a way to fix it without contacting him. If *Andras* managed to get things in hand without causing chaos, I sure hope you can."

Andras, unsure whether the comment had been a compliment or an insult, chose to believe the former and thanked the Lightbringer, whose lack of response made him swiftly reconsider.

"That man is going through the most wicked turmoil, and that endangers both him and us. If he just disappears, or worse, shows up as the next macabre display of Andras' violence, those friends are going to start looking for answers, and then you have a snowball thundering down a hill towards you that you cannot stop. You made this mess, and I expect you to clean up every last drop, because regardless of your epithets, Lawless One, Without a Master, while you are on this side of the veil in the name of this mission, you obey *me*."

Before Belial could respond, Lucifer turned abruptly and strode back into the light behind him. The gold motifs on his cloak shimmered and spread out as if infused with the essence of the radiance itself, and as he walked towards the window, his very silhouette appeared to melt into the light.

Belial and Andras stood side by side, watching silently as the Emperor's figure gradually

dissipated into the receding sunray until he vanished completely from view.

CHAPTER TEN

However, as time marched on relentlessly, as it ever does, the relatively small problem of a man who knew more than he should became entirely insignificant. The world was staring blankly in the face of what was increasingly obviously a worsening crisis.

The demons, along with a host of other ancient beings with an intimate connection to the natural world, had watched with growing concern for some time as humanity continued its reckless exploitation of the planet, but the situation now carried an unprecedented urgency. They had seen civilizations rise and fall, ecosystems flourish and collapse, but never before had they witnessed such widespread destruction wrought by one species.

In a deeply sobering moment, even Leviathan, the timeless ruler of the ocean's unfathomable depths, raised his colossal head above the surface for the first time in eight centuries.

His scales, dark and iridescent, shimmered under the moonlight, casting an ethereal glow across the turbulent waters. The behemoth's eyes, deep and primordial, bore the weight of eons as he conveyed a dire message to his Emperor.

His voice, unused for ages, was a tremor that resounded through the waves, rumbling with a mere scintilla of the fury he struggled to contain. His seas, once brimming with vibrant life and mysteries untold, now churned with a foreboding inevitability. The balance had been disrupted, and the oceans, in their growing wrath, threatened to rise and consume everything in their path. Coastal cities, with their looming buildings and hectic harbors, faced imminent doom. Island nations, cradles of unique cultures and histories, stood on the brink of annihilation, their existence obliviously perched on the edge of oblivion.

As the thalassic goliath told of the swelling tides and the encroaching waters, the grievous reality of the situation slowly became clear. The ocean, once a sanctuary for a myriad of life forms, now mirrored the tumultuous downward spiral of the world above. The unceasing rise in temperature, pollution, and human interference had turned his home into a destructive force that threatened to wipe entire civilizations from the pages of history.

The indomitable heart of Leviathan ached with both grief for what had already been lost and knowledge of what stood to be further destroyed. His coral reef gardens, vibrant and bursting with life for thousands of years, were now bleached and barren. Marine creatures, once abundant and shimmering in every color imaginable, had dwindled in numbers, their habitats and food sources ravaged by the warming waters. Even the great sea beasts, Leviathan's kin, had retreated into the deepest abysses, fleeing the inhospitable surface.

His distress was palpable as he admitted that even his immense power was now barely enough to hold back the encroaching tides. The seas, once his domain, had become a volatile and merciless adversary.

The serpent's lament was a clarion call that demanded to be heeded, painting a grim picture of the future. *"The ancient lands, and all their history and lore,"* he warned, *"risk being submerged forever, their lives and stories lost to these depths."*

In the swishing echoes of his warning, King Belial, among his epithets Lord Of The Earth, surveyed a similar decline in his own dominion. The ancient eyes that had once filled with pride at the sight of endless verdant expanses now gazed upon a scarred and fragmented landscape. The forests, his sanctuary and throne, were being ravaged by the hands of the very beings who consciously depended on their presence.

Belial stood amidst the greenery of his jungly office, looking around at the perfectly curated selection of his most cherished flora. Vines now found only on uninhabited islands draped lazily from the ceiling, and rare orchids bloomed as if in vibrant defiance of the contrasting concrete jungle outside. Here, within these walls, he could almost convince himself that the world was still as it should be. But even the peace his green haven brought him could not silence the truth that weighed heavily on his spirit.

For beyond the sanctuary of his office, he knew that the sonorous symphony of insect life and amphibians that once filled the air with their vibrant calls had grown ominously quiet over the years. The forests that had long bristled with creatures had become eerily silent, a mournful testament to the relentless march of human progress. The trees, ancient sentinels that had stood for centuries, were being felled at an alarming rate. Each timber giant that crashed to the ground in the name of money marked not only a needless loss of life but the severing of an ageless connection that bound the earth to its inhabitants.

Belial struggled to understand; the trees that humans cut down for their insatiable hunger for *more* were the very same that breathed life into their world. They were the lungs of the earth. They sustained countless lives and offered a final resting place, returning the vessel of every departed soul to the cradle of nature. Yet, in their blind pursuit of wealth, humans continued destroying them, ignorant - perhaps wilfully - of the catastrophe they were hastening.

The forest fires were the worst part. There was a point not so long ago when they were rare - freak accidents caused by nature. The news that he curated and distributed in his time as Matt Bellisle now told almost weekly of infernos that devoured everything in their path; plants, animals, and human settlements alike. The smoke of the fires carried the ashes of countless lives, carrying the scent of sorrow and despair on the wind. If he listened to those stories for too long, Belial could feel the agony of the trees as they burned, their life essence scorched away, leaving only charred husks in their wake.

He knew that as a protector of the Earth, his duty extended far beyond quiet lamentation. He needed to find a way to protect the remaining forests, tending them with the same dedication he bestowed upon his beloved office sanctuary. He had often walked through groves, his mere presence a balm to the ailing flora. Where his hand touched, new shoots sprang forth, and the earth seemed to breathe easier, if only for a moment. But now, the ruination was too widespread and too far gone, and he had to admit that his hands were as good as tied.

The king's heart pined for the balance that had been lost. He recalled a time that, on the grand scale of everything, he would consider very recent. It was a time when humans cherished nature above all else. They adored the forests, understanding their irreplaceable roles in the world and thanking them with reverence. Now, they wielded a seemingly unstoppable ax of destruction.

Belial closed his eyes and thought of his most ancient oaks, struggling to hang on, their branches reaching skyward like pleading arms. He vowed to protect them, and to nurture every tiny seedling and everything in between, with everything he was and everything he had.

He opened his eyes again and gazed first upon the green refuge of his office, and then outward, to the neon lights, gray blocks, and neverending stream of honking cars. Imbued with renewed purpose, King Belial stood tall, determined to restore the balance that had been so painfully disrupted.

It could no longer be ignored that the planet which was once a hospitable haven grew increasingly uninhabitable with each passing year. Rising temperatures scorched the land as if the world itself had been bound to Icarus' Sundial by its own occupants, melting glaciers and setting woodland aflame. The demons understood the delicate balance of nature, and they saw how the heedless actions of man were pushing the Earth towards a tipping point of no return. And for them, beings who relied on human belief to sustain themselves, there was a deeper level of threat. Not only were humans blindly driving countless animal species to extinction, they were also jeopardizing their own existence… and, albeit inadvertently, that of the demons.

Unable to look away any longer, they foresaw a future where humans, in their blind pursuit of materials that would long outlast them, would unwittingly bring about their own downfall. And with them, gods, angels and demons would be dragged down, unable to survive in a world devoid of faith.

And so, in whispered conversations and shadowed meetings across realms unseen by mortal eyes, demons on both sides of the veil debated their next move. Some advocated for intervention, believing that only they possessed the power and foresight to halt humanity's self-destructive path. Others cautioned against direct interference, fearing the violent repercussions of revealing their existence prematurely. Yet, as the Earth's cries grew louder and the signs of impending catastrophe multiplied, they all knew one thing: that time was running out.

They began to lay plans, drawing upon ancient knowledge and arcane power. They forged alliances and prepared for a decision that would alter the course of history. For they understood that the fate of humanity and their own intertwined destinies hung in a delicate balance, and the time was fast approaching when they would have to emerge from the shadows to safeguard the future of both worlds.

"Let's frame the Eat The Rich Killer shit as Satanic

sacrifices, then they'll believe in us. Nothing like a Satanic panic to bring demons to the front of everybody's mind," suggested a grinning Andras in one such meeting. His suggestion drew a chorus of emphatic noes from Belial, Crocell, and the rest of the small gathering of still-masked entities in his spacious waterfront penthouse. The space was decorated entirely in a deep wine red with unsettlingly lifelike wood carvings of deer heads staring sinisterly from every wall.

"Absolutely not," reiterated Dani Talamillo firmly. Dani, self-described "psychotherapist and marriage counselor to the stars", was better known to his allies as Duke Dantalion, a sage keeper of wisdom with an unmatched ability to understand and control human emotion, and the room fell silent to listen to him speak.

He stood a square six inches taller than Andras, clad in a black three-piece suit that almost matched the deep shade of his skin. His hair was styled in dense locs, and his piercing blue eyes contrasted sharply with his ebony complexion, holding an icy gravitas as he looked down at Andras. "We already had one human find out about us. Now take a moment to imagine the fallout if another gets a peek through the veil after that. It's bad enough that they already think the word *daemon* means *evil*, being outed as demons in the midst of a Satanic panic would endanger us all and everything we're working for."

"Thank you for being the voice of reason once again, my love," smiled Crocell, placing an arm around the waist of her inamorato as conversation resumed, ideas and scenarios bouncing off the burgundy walls.

Throughout the night, those conversations continued, ideas being harpooned just as quickly as they were floated. And in the weeks that followed, such conversations echoed through the ethereal realms and the hidden corners of mortal cities, debates ignited and extinguished like fleeting sparks in the darkness, no consensus being reached. On the other side of the veil, voices clamored desperately, seeking the safest path forward through the fragile balance of caution and cruciality.

In the glorious deserts of a pocket of time and space known as Djinnistan, a realm existing just beyond the edge of mortal comprehension, a council was convened by King Paimon. Their kingdom was a place of mirage-like beauty, where endless shimmering dunes, sculpted by unseen winds, glowed golden under a sun that never seemed to set, casting a perpetual twilight over the realm.

This particular gathering was held in a courtyard adorned with towering limestone pillars, each carved with intricate patterns and symbols from civilizations long forgotten by the human world. The walls, too, bore primeval etchings, stories of gods and heroes, battles and victories, all etched with painstaking detail. The limestone, white and beige, seemed to drink in the sunlight, its surface warm and inviting.

And amidst the ancient grandeur, nature's touch was vibrantly present - bougainvillea shrubs, their deep pinkish-red blooms a striking contrast to the pale stone, climbed the walls and wound around the pillars. Their petals fluttered gently in the breeze, adding a touch of wild beauty to the structured elegance of the courtyard.

As the council gathered, the air was filled with a sense of gravitas and anticipation. The scent of white musk, rich and exotic, wafted through the courtyard, mingling with the earthy aroma of the desert. Djinnistan was a place where time seemed to stand still, where past and present melded seamlessly, and the future was yet to be written.

Among the proposals of *how* to write it was a particularly bold one - to form an alliance with Cypress and have him gather a following - and it was gaining momentum like wildfire on a dry wind. Growing numbers of demons argued passionately for the plan, citing Cypress's solitude and gradual descent into the quicksand of madness as fertile ground for their plot to have him form a Luciferian cult. "He is already estranged from his kind," cried an anguished Prince Beelzebub to a collective murmur of approval. "He could be our voice among the humans who may still believe, rallying them around us!"

Suddenly, amidst the fervor, Paimon's voice cut through the tumult with unwavering authority. Their gaze, penetrating and seemingly omniscient, held the assembly in a respectful lull. "Not a chance," they pronounced pointedly. "Cypress is trying to move on. We must allow him to do so and find his own path. To embroil him in our game plan is to court disaster, it's a mistake King Belial already made and one the Emperor will not allow us to repeat."

The hush that followed was broken by Prince Belphegor, a short but tremendously wide individual with a deep burbling voice. He rose to his feet, a rare occurrence by all accounts, looking markedly out of place in a slightly-too-small slate gray tracksuit. "Beelzebub is right; the plan may be risky, but doing nothing risks our very existence," he countered, his voice resonating with defiance. "We need allies on the other side of the veil. Real allies, who know who we are. Cypress could be the key to finding them and awakening their allegiance!"

"To manipulate Cypress in such a manner is to gamble with forces beyond our control," Paimon insisted, their tone allowing no space for further dissent. "Let him find his way back to his path and walk it in peace. The Emperor's word is final."

With the option of involving Cypress in their plans now firmly dismissed, the council of demons reached a reluctantly unanimous decision to continue their clandestine existence on the mortals' side of the veil. The precariousness of their situation presented a need for patience that could even be seen as conflicting, and by embracing human forms, they could blend into society and fight for the world the only way they could safely do so - as its mere inhabitants.

They knew well the power of myth and legend - through art, music, and storytelling, they could subtly weave threads of their existence into the fabric of human consciousness, using the ephemeral realm of pop culture as a subtle conduit to keep alive the faint embers of recognition.

In the desert courtyard where they had convened, echoes of ancient vows resonated with a solemn determination. They would walk among mortals, their true nature concealed beneath human guises, subtly guiding the world towards a path that aligned with their own timeless purposes.

And if and when the time came for them to do so, they would slip effortlessly back through the veil that separated their realms, as countless deities had done before.

CHAPTER ELEVEN

The thing about secret conversations held in the shadows is that there is invariably a separate conversation, even more covert, held in an even darker shadow afterward. The negotiations between the demons were no exception, and within hours of King Paimon's refusal to allow them to manipulate Cypress Rafferty as their puppet, Princes Belphegor and Beelzebub had quietly made their way to visit the one ally they knew they could count on to support them.

The brothers, though often considered synonymous with sloth and gluttony, were formidably resourceful and relentless in their ambitions, now more than ever. They moved through the hidden realms with the silence and precision of shadows themselves, heading towards a place where the light of day never reached, where morality was optional (and frankly frowned upon) and the darkest of secrets were the threads of the very fabric of existence. There, in the heart of darkness, they found who they were looking for.

The meeting took place in a hidden chamber lost to time, obscured by layers of long-forgotten spells to ensure it remained invisible unless its resident wished otherwise.

The air was thick with the scent of brimstone and incense, the walls adorned with arcane symbols that seemed to pulse with a faint, eerie glow.

As Belphegor and Beelzebub made their case, the chamber seemed to shrink around them, the suffocating atmosphere coating every word. They spoke passionately of the need for action, of the perilous state of their world, and most importantly, of the necessity of using Cypress as a catalyst for change.

Their intended ally listened intently, weighing their words with a shrewdness that could only have been honed through millennia of scheming. This was a being who understood the delicate dance of power and the importance of choosing the right moment to strike. The silence that followed their plea was thick with anticipation.

Then, finally, he spoke. "Are you *entirely sure* this is what you want to do?"

They knew that every word was loaded with distrust, the following pause a measure of their determination.

Belphegor and Beelzebub, undeterred, answered in the affirmative with a pure zeal that matched their desperation, and in the end, their ally nodded slowly, the flicker of a smile crossing the corners of his lips.

"Very well," he mused. "You have my support."

And that was that. The pact was made, the course was set. The Princes knew that their path would be fraught with danger and opposition, but they also knew that they had taken the first crucial step towards their goal.

As they departed the chamber, the shadows swept out with them, swirling around their bodies as if to shroud them from prying eyes. They moved with purpose, their resolve strengthened by the knowledge that they were not alone in their quest. Belphegor and Beelzebub, along with their newfound leader, finally felt ready to challenge the status quo and carve out a new destiny for themselves and their kind. And the darkness itself held its breath, waiting for the first move in a game that would change everything.

"Paimon!" declared Beelzebub after a while of walking in silence back towards the courtyard.

"What about them?" asked his brother, dogged by a sneaking suspicion but hoping for a different answer.

"We need them, Belph. They're the keeper of secrets. They can reveal everything to Cypress, and then to his members. They can make sure anyone who tries to cast those secrets upon the wrong ears can't do so. We need to get them on side."

Belphegor groaned in exasperation. "Somehow I knew you were going to say that, and yet I wanted *so damn bad* to be wrong. We can't tell Paimon about this, Beelz."

"You know they'll find out anyway, right? Again, keeper of secrets and all that."

"Duh. But by that time, it'll be too late for them to stop us. Telling them *before* we go will screw up the whole plan. We're not telling Paimon."

Suddenly, a voice rang from behind a stone pillar. "Not telling Paimon *what*, exactly?"

The Princes swore quietly under their breaths in unison as King Paimon swept into the open, silken robes of burnt orange and deep magenta fluttering behind them in the desert wind.

"Well, you wanted to open your stupid mouth. Here's your chance," spat Belphegor, eliciting a dark glare from the bug-like eyes of his brother.

Beelzebub stepped forward, his tall, gangly frame accentuated by the long pinstripe jacket he wore over his all-black outfit. "We need your help, Your Majesty," he began, but Paimon cut him off immediately.

"Whatever is going on here, dearies, I can almost guarantee you have no chance of enlisting my help. So let's skip the pitch and get right to what it was you were planning to conceal from me, shall we?"

"Yes, of course," laughed Beelzebub nervously, glancing at his brother for reassurance but being met only with a look that seemed to say *"You made your bed, now lie in it."*

Beelzebub turned back toward Paimon and conveyed to them the firm belief of the Princes that Cypress was their only hope. He explained how, in as respectful a defiance as possible against the decrees of both Paimon and Emperor Lucifer, they intended to proceed with their plans to establish Cypress as a cult leader, but the success of the plot depended on Paimon themself.

"I've made my position abundantly clear," Paimon told him bluntly when he was finished with his speech. "If it somehow wasn't clear enough, I hope this will be: *I will not support this plan. What's more, I will actively work against any efforts to pursue it.* Is that understood?"

The conversation that followed between Beelzebub and Paimon was charged with tension, the air around them thick with unspoken implications louder than their murmured words. Beelzebub's conviction was palpable, radiating from him like a dark aura. He believed with all his soul, no matter how misguidedly, that Cypress was the key to their salvation. The notion of using someone with such an unresisting blend of madness and knowledge to gather human followers, to harness the collective energy of belief and devotion, was one he refused to let go of without a fight.

Paimon, however, saw the situation very differently. They viewed the use of Cypress as not only cruel and dangerous but also unnecessary. Their wisdom, cultivated by overseeing entire epochs of human existence, told them that forcing such a path could lead to catastrophic consequences. Their refusal was more than a matter of principle; it was a strategic decision to maintain the delicate balance that existed between the two sides of the veil.

They also understood the ramifications of allowing Cypress to ascend as a cult leader, something they implored the Princes to understand. They warned of the potential for all-out chaos, for the destabilization of society on both sides of the veil. The delicate equilibrium that had been maintained for so long had already been jeopardized by Cypress' unpredictable meddling, and Paimon was determined to stop it from happening again.

The monarch swooped away with the wind as quickly as they'd arrived, and Belphegor and Beelzebub lingered for a moment in their wake, silent, a sense of foreboding hanging over them. They already knew that the path they had chosen was fraught with peril, but Paimon had made it clear that the lack of their support made it even more treacherous. Despite that, though, the brothers were undeterred. They were prepared to forge ahead, driven by a conviction that this was the only way to ensure their survival and eventual return to greatness.

In the aftermath of the confrontation, the undercurrents of rebellion and ambition began to ripple through the courts of the Underworld. Whispers of the Princes' plans had begun to circulate, stirring both support and opposition among their peers. By morning, the seeds of dissent were well and truly sown, the stage set for a struggle that would test the limits of power and loyalty.

The first to approach the Princes directly, perhaps unsurprisingly, was Andras.

"Is it true that you have the support of the Dark One?" he asked, and Belphegor nodded smugly in response.

"We visited Lord Lucifuge in the hours after the council, yes," said Beelzebub. "He is convinced, as we are, that this is the way forward, and offered us his full support."

"Good," breathed Andras with a dark smile. "Support as a sentimental concept could not mean less to me, but it's good to know you two asshats aren't running the show."

"Now, now, Andras, there's no need for that, is there?" called a crow that had been watching from the top of one of the courtyard's many ornate turrets.

Andras looked up, rolling his eyes when he caught sight of the corvid. "Get down from there, Malphas, and talk with us like a man," he taunted, and the crow spread its wings, plunging downward towards them. It landed a few pecks on the heads and shoulders of the three men before settling, hitting the ground not as a bird but as a pale man with a hooked nose and long black hair, dressed in a military uniform of midnight blue and white gold.

"I just wanted to hear it for myself. You know, that the plans are real, that it's really happening," he explained. "I'm glad to see that it is. For what it's worth, I'm with you."

Neither of the three was willing to feed his ego by saying it aloud, but it was worth a lot. President Malphas, renowned for his ability to form armies and unite artificers from all corners of the world, was perhaps the most valuable ally a plot based on forming cults could hope for.

"When do you plan to make contact?" he asked.

Before Belphegor or Beelzebub could answer, Andras interjected with a grin, his tone dripping with morbid anticipation. "Why wait any longer? They were just leaving now."

Meanwhile, through an ever-thinning veil, Cypress

Rafferty enjoyed his last moments of oblivious bliss. He wandered through the aisles of his local grocery store with a new sense of appreciation for the dated mundanity of it, finally feeling free of (or at least able to ignore) the constant gnawing sense of unease that had plagued him for so long. As he reached for a bag of oranges, he collided with a large meaty arm that almost caused him to lose his grip on his groceries.

"Watch it, dumbass," Cypress muttered. Instantly regretting his outburst, he stepped back to apologize but stopped short as he took in the man's appearance. He was enormous, his frame dominating the narrow aisle. His face was round and flushed, glistening with sweat, but his eyes were sharp and intelligent.

"My deepest apologies," the man said, his grumbly voice sweetened by a saccharine kindness that seemed disingenuous. "Allow me to introduce myself. Prince Belphegor, at your service."

Before Cypress could react, he heard a faint buzzing, growing louder by the second. He looked up to see a swarm of small black flies swirling above him, coalescing into the shape of a tall, lanky man as they settled. The buzzing subsided, replaced by a low chuckle as the figure solidified, his eyes twinkling with an emotion Cypress was unable to recognize.

"And *I*," the man said, "am his older brother, Prince Beelzebub."

Cypress's heart raced. *Not this. Not again.* He had read their names, acknowledged the likelihood that they were real and possibly somewhere not far away. But them being right there, in the flesh, was a different matter entirely.

"What do you want from me?" moaned Cypress, feeling himself being dragged back into the darkness he'd fought so hard to work his way out of. "I started painting again. My art is selling better than ever, so well that I was almost thankful for the inspiration. My life is just getting back on track, what could possibly be so important that y'all have to show up here and stomp all over it again?"

"We need your help," Belphegor said, his voice losing its faux softness and gaining a threatening edge. "We need you to spread the word. The only way that we all survive - that's you lot and us - is if our messages can be relayed directly to the people on this side of the veil. And you know how we can do that? CULTS!"

The last word was accompanied by a dramatic jazz hands gesture, leaving Cypress dazed by incredulity. "Wait, what?" he balked. "You can't seriously be asking me to start a goddamn cult."

Beelzebub laughed, ruffling Cypress' hair. "Love the choice of words, Cy... goddamn cult. A cult in reverence of those damned by religion, I daresay, would quite *literally* be a goddamn cult. So, yes, that's precisely what we're telling you to start."

"Yeah," Belphegor growled. "Telling, not asking. Lord Andras is counting on your support, too."

"Andras?"

Cypress felt a chill run down his spine. The thought of aligning with the being he knew as Bill Anderson was horrifying. The thought of defying him was tenfold more.

"You have a choice, Rafferty," Belphegor said, stepping closer, the sweet smell of decay that seemed to cling to him mingling with the stench of sweat. "Find a way to spread the word, or be a coward and keep it to yourself. But remember, Andras don't take kindly to cowardice, and nor do we."

Cypress was torn, the weight of the Princes' words pressing down on him, suffocating him. He wanted to scream, to run, to hide, but he knew none of that would make a blind bit of difference.

Belphegor, sensing his hesitation, suddenly grew aggressive. "Do you comprehend what's at stake here, or are you really as stupid and useless as you look?" he snarled, his face contorting with rage. Without thinking, Cypress raised the can of beans he was still holding in his left hand and launched it in Belphegor's direction. It connected with his face with a sickening crack, and although apparently physically unharmed the demon reeled, clearly unaccustomed to bodily confrontation.

Realizing his mistake, Cypress turned to run, but his feet felt like they were glued to the floor. He panicked as he tried over and over to lift his feet from the floor, but remained rooted to the spot, completely frozen.

Belphegor, who had now recovered, glowered at the paralyzed man, beady eyes blazing with rage. "You'd do well to remember who's in control here," he hissed. A spark of light illuminated him for a second, and then, as if by magic - and perhaps it really was - he was gone.

Beelzebub stood there for a moment longer, his lanky frame casting an elongated shadow across the aisle. He seemed to hesitate, his gaze fixed on Cypress with an intensity that suggested he wanted to say something more. Cypress watched, still frozen, as a fleeting look of regret crossed his face before he offered a small, almost apologetic smile.

Ultimately without uttering another word, the demon's body began to splinter, dissolving into a cloud of flies right before Cypress's eyes. The insects were buzzing around in a frantic dance, the air thick with their presence, when one particularly bold fly landed on Cypress's nose. Instinctively, he swatted it away, and in that instant, he realized he could move again and whispered his bewildered thanks.

He watched, both mesmerized and horrified, as the swarm of flies formed a writhing black mass that surged toward a nearby vent. They seemed to move with purpose, disappearing into the darkness one by one until the last of them vanished from sight. And Cypress simply stood, still just inches away from the oranges he'd innocently reached for what seemed like an eternity ago, breathing heavily as he tried his best to process the bizarre encounter. He stared at the vent, half expecting the flies to reappear, or worse, a barn owl to burst through the grate.

He took a shaky step forward, the reality of his situation slowly sinking in. The memory of Belphegor's hostility and Beelzebub's hesitant smile haunted his mind. He knew that he himself was a mere fly, caught in a web even more dangerous and complex than he had ever imagined, and wondered if he'd be better off welcoming the sweet release of the spider's fangs.

Eventually, the harrowing sound of a woman bawling brought him back to lucidity, and he spun around to face the front of the store. The two young cashiers, having witnessed the strange scene, were panicking. The wailing girl and her terrified boyfriend, neither older than twenty-one, clung to each other's faded red uniforms, babbling incoherently through tears. Cypress walked towards them slowly, hands raised to show that he posed no threat.

"What the hell was *that?*" the young woman screamed, eyeing him fearfully.

"I don't know," he lied, his voice trembling. "I just... I don't know."

But deep down, he knew. And the knowledge was a heavy burden, one he was less sure than ever that he could bear alone.

CHAPTER TWELVE

Though Belphegor and Beelzebub had retreated to the shadows, the furor had only just begun, being as it was that they were no longer alone in their audacity. The lower-ranking demons, emboldened by their show, began to breach the veil with increasing frequency. They appeared in buzzing city streets, quiet suburban parks, and crowded shopping malls, revealing their true names and performing feats of magic that left onlookers baffled and intrigued. Most people, fortunately, dismissed them as oddballs and illusionists, their tricks as elaborate acts.

One evening, a man with long, thick red hair and eyes like burning coals stood on a bustling corner in Times Square. His presence was magnetic, drawing curious glances as he began juggling balls of fire that defied the laws of physics. The flames danced and twirled in the air, moving with a sentient grace that hinted at something far beyond mere illusion. As a crowd gathered, their faces illuminated by the flickering embers, he revealed his name to be Pyronus. He claimed to be the son of a great Earl of the Underworld, and the people laughed and cheered and laughed some more, enchanted by what they believed to be part of an eccentric show. But Cypress, watching from the street corner, knew better. He felt a cold dread seep into his bones, recognizing the dark truth behind the man's blazing performance.

Not far away, beneath the tremendous oaks of Central Park, an unnaturally tall woman with skin like midnight silk and hair that shimmered like starlight stood proudly. She called herself Mahalath, and she sang, her voice a melody of long-unheard tongues that echoed through the twilight. With fluid movements of her wrists, she summoned what she claimed were departed souls - shadows that danced and twisted at her command, forming shapes that defied logic and nature.

The jaded citizens of New York City, having long since had their bellyful of the constant barrage of street performers, grumbled as they walked past, oblivious. Tourists, however, were captivated. They clapped and tossed coins at her bare feet, clueless to the true nature of what they were witnessing - a display of necromancy - raw, ancient magic that had been confined to another world for centuries.

Cypress watched the scenes unfold through videos on his phone, his heart pounding with a mixture of fear and fascination. The city, usually a fortress of commercial falsity and human indifference, had seemed to pulse with a strange energy for some time, but now similar footage was popping up from all over the world. London, Berlin, Paris, Zagreb, all gazed on in awe of these wonderful new performers on their streets.

What they didn't know was that the appearance of these beings, openly flaunting their supernatural abilities, was a sign. A sign that the veil between worlds was thinning, that the old powers were growing restless.

As he walked towards the subway station, ducking through the throngs of people, Cypress couldn't shake the feeling that he was being watched. Every face in the crowd seemed like a potential threat, every shadow a lurking danger. He knew that the demons were becoming bolder, their presence more overt. The streets of the world's leading cities, with their constant hum of life and movement, had become a stage for ancient beings long thought to be myths. And as the sole guardian of the truth, Cypress had never felt more alone.

Each step he took was heavy with the weight of impending chaos. The city's bright lights and endless noise felt oppressive, a raucous racket that masked the whispers of the supernatural weaving through the air. His mind raced, filled with thoughts of how to protect himself, how to warn others, if he should at all, and most of all, how to find a way to survive in a world that was rapidly slipping out of the grasp of reason.

His sense of unease grew with each passing day. Every stranger he passed on the street, every face in the crowd, could be a demon in disguise. Paranoia haunted him, and he found himself glancing over his shoulder constantly, searching for any sign of the supernatural.

Nights were the worst. Cypress would sit in his dimly lit room, eyes fixed on the door, ears straining for the faintest sound of a knock. His heart would race at the slightest creak of the floorboards or the distant hum of the elevator. He barely slept, afraid that the moment he closed his eyes, a swarm of flies would buzz from beneath his bed, manifesting into Beelzebub staring down at him. He started to see shadows where there were none, silhouettes moving past his 29th-floor window, taunting him from the periphery of his vision.

One night, the paranoia reached a fever pitch. Cypress sat in his usual spot, a kitchen knife that he knew would be useless should his fears come true clutched tightly in his hand. His eyes were bloodshot from lack of sleep, and every muscle in his body was tense. He stared at the door, willing it to stay shut, but fearing it would burst from the hinges at any moment revealing the hulking frame of Belphegor, or creak open to show Andras' wolf creeping in, its master on its back with a sadistic grin and a sledgehammer. The minutes ticked by agonizingly slowly, each one stretching sluggishly into the next.

Suddenly, a noise shattered the silence. Cypress jumped out of bed, heart pounding, then realized that it was just the wind rattling the window. He took a deep breath, trying in vain to calm himself, but the fear that something malevolent was always lurking just out of sight, waiting for the perfect moment to strike, remained.

As dawn broke, the first rays of sunlight piercing through the curtains, Cypress finally allowed himself to relax. Once again, nothing had happened. He hadn't been attacked, but the threat felt no less real. He refused to let himself settle into a false sense of security again. He knew that the demons were growing bolder, and it was only a matter of time before one of them made their move.

What he didn't know, much to his distress, was what exactly that move would be.

The moment that realization dawned on him was much like

any other. As he passed through the crowded subway station, he noticed a young demon brazenly turning rats into puffs of smoke, their squeaks cut short by sudden, magical explosions. The air smelled faintly of sulfur, and the passengers nearby either ignored the spectacle or dismissed it as another street magician's distasteful trick.

But for Cypress, it was an epiphanous wake-up call. If so many demons were descending on New York City, presenting their powers so openly, then there was a good chance he could find the very one he needed: *Paimon.*

He boarded the subway, heading with purpose towards Times Square. He pushed through the throngs of people, ignoring their disgruntled shouts, making a beeline towards Antonio's hot dog stand. "Tony," he called as he got closer. "Have you seen them?"

The older man, in the middle of preparing two hot dogs for a young tourist couple, shot him a confused look. After serving his customers, he turned towards Cypress. "Slow down, man, what's the rush? Have I seen who?"

"Paimon- I mean Tai, Taina. The person with the scarves. I need a scarf. I need a damn scarf, bro, now."

Tony shook his head morosely. "I told you not to dig into it, Cowboy. I knew there was somethin' spooky going on. You dug anyway, didn't you?"

"Alright, I dug," admitted Cypress. "I really wish I hadn't, and I think the only way outta the hole I done dug is with one of them scarves."

"They're down that way," gestured Antonio. "Keep

walking past the Italian place and you'll see 'em on the corner."

Cypress planted a kiss on Antonio's wrinkled forehead, as surprised by his own gesture as its recipient was, and took off towards Tai's stall.

As he walked, his mind raced, thoughts swirling like the eddies of a storm. The city seemed to blur around him, the faces of strangers morphing into a faceless mass, their conversations melting into an indistinct hum. His heart pounded in his chest as he replayed the scenes of recent weeks over and over in his head - Belphegor and Beelzebub in the grocery store, the growing number of demons who followed suit, their brazen displays of power, *the creeping sense of dread that had taken root in his soul*. This city - no, this world - was on the brink of something terrible, and he was tired of being caught in the middle of it.

Finally, the unsettlingly familiar smell of orange blossom and vanilla told him he was close to his port of call, and as he turned the corner, he saw it. The stall. His shimmering, silken salvation. He stood for a few seconds, just watching Tai, taking in everything they did and everything they truly were for the first time, until their voice pulled him from his trance. "Following me around again, sweetpea?" they called out with a grin. "You know you could just ask me out for dinner?"

Cypress smiled back at them, his first genuine smile since being pulled back into the unknown by Belphegor and Beelzebub. Maybe it was the relief of being recognized and not chastised for his stunt in Vegas, or perhaps it was just the knowledge that his nightmare would soon be over - all he knew was that he was damn happy to see them. "This Italian place right there *does* smell pretty delicious," he admitted. "Maybe if I find you again after you do me this favor, I'll do that."

Tai approached him slowly, their smile fading as a look of concern grew on their face. "Which favor, Cypress? I'm not in the business of doing favors for free. Especially not for... well, you know."

"For humans," sighed Cypress quietly.

"Precisely. All magic comes at a price."

"Respectfully, friend, I think I've paid the price ten times over then some," said Cypress, his voice growing more insistent. "I'll admit that it was my mistake to start digging into this... following you, bothering King Belial, all of it. But I've paid my dues. I lost the woman I loved. I lost my friends. I lost my job. The grocery store is closed because two of your henchmen showed up and sent one cashier on the run and the other into a psych ward, because of me. If I ain't paid the price, then the price is too damn high."

Paimon gazed at him sympathetically, taking in every word. "First of all," they said, taking his hand and leading him into the back of the stall away from the ears of passers-by, "Princes Belphegor and Beelzebub are in no way my henchmen, and I'm frankly insulted that you'd think I was behind such reckless buffoonery. The unrest is not confined to this side of the veil, dearie."

Cypress stammered an apology, which was graciously

accepted as the demon moved swiftly on to their next point: "I'm willing to consider your argument that your sacrifices have already been made. So tell me, what manner of favor do you need from me?"

"I heard the story about the kid you saved... the monster who got shot, you know the one I mean. And when I started looking into all of this, the demonolatry stuff, *you*, I found out how you do it. You have power over secrets. You enchant the scarves somehow to reveal secrets and make them known, right?"

Paimon's unbothered silence was both an affirmation and an invitation to continue.

"You also mentioned being able to make sure secrets never come from under the rug, or somethin' like that. Does that mean you could - hypothetically - also make a scarf that makes someone forget a secret?"

Paimon let out a soft laugh, finally understanding Cypress' intention.

"You want me to *Eternal Sunshine* you!"

"You what?" asked Cypress, perplexed and mildly concerned at the ominous sound of the phrase. It sounded like a euphemism for death - an option he'd given long thought to in the dark hours of sleepless nights, but deep down hoped was at least Plan B.

"It's a movie, honey, don't look at me like that!" the djinn laughed with a smile that could only be described as tender. "I'm not gonna hurt you. I didn't want you mixed up in this in the first place. The movie is about a couple who need to forget each other so that they can move on, live their lives, and be happy. So they go to a doctor who can wipe all memories of the other person and the relationship from their brains. That's what you want."

"Yes!" cried Cypress, resisting the urge to whoop with joy. "That is exactly what I want. Make sure I know nothing about any of this. No demons, no veils, no magic. Let me start to live again. Maybe I'll move back to Texas, and help my dad on the ranch like he always wanted. Who knows? I just wanna find out where life takes me without… this."

Paimon stood in silence for a few moments, contemplating the crossroads in front of them.

If they granted Cypress his wish, he'd be free. Not only that, but the demons' secrets would remain veiled. He would no longer be a threat, his knowledge erased, his memories shrouded in the folds of the scarf. But they couldn't ignore the fact that their act of mercy could come at a steep cost for their own kind. Without Cypress, the last tenuous link between worlds could collapse - not to mention that any iteration of Belphegor and Beelzebub's plan was firmly off the table, forever, even if it eventually turned out to be the right course of action.

Paimon twisted and twirled a scarf in their hands, letting it flow between them like glimmering emerald green water. Cypress recognized the intricate patterns of golden birds and leaves, realizing that he hadn't noticed that first day how beautiful they were. It was a piece of delicate craftsmanship, each thread woven with care, infused with magic and meaning.

The truth was that Paimon had known, from the moment they laid eyes on Cypress, that this scarf was destined for him. But its true significance had been a mystery even to them back then, a curious intuition that had now crystallized into stark clarity.

As the scarf wound around their hands, the golden birds seemed to come alive, fluttering against the lush green background. The leaves rustled as if stirred by an invisible breeze, a silent reminder of the interconnectedness of all things. Cypress stared in awe, aware that the scarf was now more than just a garment; it was a symbol of choices and consequences, one small stitch in the cosmic drapery of destiny.

Paimon, meanwhile, closed their eyes, allowing themself to feel the full weight of their role as a ruler, as a guardian of secrets and harbinger of fate. The decision was not simply a case of one man's freedom or the success of a singular plan; it was about the balance between worlds, the raveled interplay of light and shadow, power and restraint.

The familiar mantle of responsibility and consequence settled upon their shoulders in a daunting reminder that the true power of a deity lies not in the weaving of magic, but in the wisdom of knowing when to use it. And Paimon knew what was good, and right. With a deep, steadying breath, they resolved to face the future, whatever it might hold, in the shadow of their decision.

They handed the scarf to Cypress silently, afraid that a word, or even a breath, on either side could tip them over the edge and make them change their mind.

"Was that… it?" asked Cypress gingerly. "What you did with your hands, was that the… is it… can I…"

"It's done," interjected Paimon. "All you have to do is put it on when you're ready, and suddenly, I'm just a very good-looking street vendor, I just gave you a scarf for free, and demons and faeries and gods are all just in the movies."

Cypress was sorely tempted to ask about the faeries and gods, and learn as much as he could before putting on the scarf and sweeping it all into oblivion. However, he knew that if he indulged his curiosity, he might not want to leave it all behind and return to a mundane world where everyday things, people, and places aren't laced with magic and meaning. So he held his tongue, and pulled Paimon into his arms, hugging them tight. He breathed in their sweet, floral scent, knowing that this was the last time he'd ever truly know them. The last time he'd ever knowingly be this close to someone of another world. And in all likelihood, though he hoped otherwise, the last time he'd ever feel this wonderstruck by another being's mere presence. "Thanks for everything, Tai," he murmured, and felt their body shake with laughter in response.

"You have the rest of your life to call me Tai if you decide to stick around," they replied, not pulling away from the embrace, allowing Cypress to drink in every moment of what would be his last encounter with magic. "Call me Paimon."

He gave them one last squeeze then stepped back, studying every detail of their robes, their beads, their face, as if determined to make the most of his final moments of orphic knowledge. "Well, then, thank you, Paimon. For a hell of an adventure, and for bringing it to a long overdue end too. Extend my thanks to King Belial, and y'all take care. That sounds real stupid, don't it? Me telling y'all to take care when you're... anyway. Good luck with everything, and I hope that when my time comes, we can meet again on the other side of the veil."

"I've no doubt of that, dearie," chuckled Paimon. "We're gonna have a lot of catching up to do after I debrief you."

"I'm looking forward to that," Cypress said, realizing only as the words left his mouth that he truly meant it.

"Don't look forward to it," Paimon urged him. "There's plenty of time. I'm going nowhere, and nor is King B. We'll be waiting. You go and live your life, help your family with the ranch, paint, drink, find love, whatever it is you have to do out there. I don't want to see you on the other side for a very long time. Okay?"

"Alright," said Cypress, looking at the floor in the hope that the demon wouldn't see the tears welling in his eyes. "Well then, I best get to gettin'. Bye, Paimon."

He didn't listen for a reply. But after taking only a few steps away, he turned back, one last question needling him. "Hey! That movie you talked about," he called, raising his voice to be heard over the cacophony of honking horns and distant chatter. "The sunshine thing. How does the movie end?"

Paimon grinned back at him. *"They find each other all over again, and get back together."*

With a polite nod, Cypress turned away again and walked, thinking about the implications of the movie ending. They wiped their memories of each other in order to move on, only to end up back in the same situation. Had something pulled them back where they were supposed to be? Would it also pull him back into this world of magic and mayhem? Does that only work when you're messing with fate? He wasn't messing with fate, after all, this was all accidental… right?

"It's just a stupid movie," he muttered to himself as he reached his subway platform. He told himself that it would work as intended; that he'd be free. He'd never have to look at the TV screen and wonder if the person on it was human, or sit awake staring at the window of his high-rise apartment expecting the silhouette of someone walking past. News would be news, music would be music, and the name Lucifer would simply be something his Mawmaw bellowed at anyone with tattoos. So why couldn't he bring himself to put on the scarf?

Biting his lip nervously, he concluded that perhaps a part of him simply didn't want to. The experience had been raw, painful and devastating. But it had also been magical, and enlightening, and given him a whole new perspective on the inner workings of every aspect of the world he lived in.

He looked down at the grimy tracks and, for a moment, seriously considered throwing the scarf down onto them. He imagined the subway coming, its steel wheels tangling and ripping the green silk, and wondered if the little gold birds would fly away, back to Paimon, twittering word of his choice in their ear.

As he wondered how Paimon would react, the subway screeched into view, its metallic caterwaul echoing through the station as the doors slid open directly in front of him.

A gaggle of tourists rushed off, their excited chatter about seeing Times Square filling the air. As they dispersed, the sea of people around him surged forward, pushing and shoving to get on board - commuters, students, giggling teenage couples, each one eager to get home. He looked around, seeing exactly what he'd been missing. The excitement that the tourists found in the bright lights of the city. The routine the locals fall into in the humdrum of daily life there. He'd forgotten what either side of that coin felt like. And in that moment, he knew what his decision would be.

As he jumped onto the subway, darting between the closing doors, he wrapped the scarf around his neck. A warm, fuzzy feeling fell over his head, reminding him of the feeling of settling in under the duvet after one too many beers. He blundered towards the nearest handrail, holding himself up as the wooziness wore off, and blinked rapidly. The world came back into view and he locked eyes with an elderly woman, laden with two large shopping bags, her brow furrowed in concern.

"You okay?" she asked, placing one bag on the ground to steady him with one hand. "You look like you might pass out. Wanna sit down?" She pointed at the seat she'd just vacated, but Cypress shook his head.

"I'm good, ma'am, thank you, though," he smiled in reply. "I think I bumped my head on the way in, somehow."

"As long as you're alright now," the lady shrugged, sinking back into her seat.

And he was. In fact, somehow, his head had never felt clearer.

CHAPTER THIRTEEN

It was not long before news of Cypress' decision reached the highest ranks on the other side of the veil. Mere minutes, in fact.

Emperor Lucifer, who had until this point been kept in the dark in hopes that the situation could be brought under control without his involvement, listened with a growing sense of fury as the tale unfolded before him. The golden motifs on his robe seemed to crackle with his anger as his eyes sparked viciously, their infernal light reflecting the tempest of emotions within him.

The tale began at the end: with Cypress having chosen to erase all knowledge of the demons and their plans from his memory. Initially, this pleased the Emperor, who assumed that Belial had given the man a persuasive nudge. But as the story continued, detailing how Belphegor and Beelzebub had accosted Cypress in broad daylight, his rage grew. He paced slowly as he took in each word, listening to how their reckless actions had set off a string of chaos that was now spiraling out of control.

Like tinder to a fire, reports of demons openly flaunting their powers flooded from a desperate Paimon's lips. They told how lower-ranking demons, encouraged by the

Princes' audacious display, had crossed the veil without permission and started performing magic in front of humans, revealing their true names and natures in a desperate bid for reverence. One thing was painfully clear to the Lightbringer. *What should have remained hidden was now dangerously close to being completely exposed.* The consequences were already evident: the two young cashiers who had witnessed the Princes' display were now left traumatized beyond repair, their lives shattered by the horrifying reality they had glimpsed.

The once subtle infiltration of the other side of the veil was openly descending into madness, and the Emperor was incandescent. He had always known that keeping the balance between worlds required a delicate touch, and it was clearly one that the Princes and their acolytes had grossly underestimated. His thoughts raced as he considered the ramifications of their actions - their reckless pursuit of power and recognition was threatening the very essence of their existence, and he knew he was now charged with stopping them.

As the final details of the uprising were relayed, Lucifer turned to face Paimon, the sheer force of his very presence dominating the room. The shadows seemed to recoil from him as if fearing his wrath, envisioning torturous punishments handed out liberally. But his decision was simple, swift and resolute: the rogue demons, those who had abandoned the subtlety and discretion required of their kind, would be exiled back behind the veil. Their reckless actions had already jeopardized too much, and he could not afford further risk.

The Lightbringer's voice, cold and commanding, bounced

sharply off the walls. "I will no longer tolerate this kind of insubordination and chaos within my ranks," he declared. Paimon signaled their agreement with a deep bow, retreating from the room backward, not out of convention but a genuine hesitancy to turn their back on the seething Emperor.

As soon as Paimon had retired out of sight, Emperor Lucifer walked slowly, steadily, toward one of the beaming rays of light shining through the stained glass windows of his great hall. The light bathed him in an ethereal glow as he moved, his presence seeming to absorb the brilliance, refracting it into dazzling prisms that danced along the stone walls. With a final, graceful stride, he stepped into the heart of the radiance and disappeared, traversing the veil between realms.

On the other side, he emerged into a dimly lit apartment where the very two men he'd been seeking were lounging, engrossed in plotting their next move to contact Cypress, evidently still unaware of the day's happenings. Prince Belphegor looked up into the round eyes of his much taller brother with a look of fear and defeat as the sunray beaming through their window materialized into the dignified figure of the Emperor. *Busted.*

"Give me a chance to explain, Your Grace," began Prince Beelzebub, but Lucifer raised a deceptively dainty hand, promptly silencing him.

"There will be *plenty* of time to explain on the other side of the veil, where you both belong, and where you'll be staying permanently," he told them through gritted teeth.

Belphegor took a knee in front of the Lightbringer, audibly struggling as he lowered his corpulent body in genuflection. "I am so terribly sorry, Your Grace," he simpered. "I tried to warn Beelzebub, but he forced me to go along with his plan. I knew it was a terrible mistake. Please allow me to stay and right his wrongs."

A disgruntled Beelzebub shouted out defensively in response, swearing gutturally at his brother before turning his own attention to the Emperor. "He's lying," he exclaimed. "We both made this plan. But it was Belphegor who got aggressive with the human and that's where it all went wrong. I should stay and handle it sensibly, as I would have if I'd come alone in the first place."

The brothers continued their heated argument, each blaming the other for their current predicament. Belphegor, despite his considerable bulk, heaved himself back to his feet to shout at his brother, the room shaking with his roaring accusations. Beelzebub, spindly and agitated, waved his long arms in frustration, his voice rising in pitch as he countered every attack. Their bickering grew louder by the second, filling the smoky room with a din of excuses and self-justifications.

Lucifer's patience quickly wore thin, and with a shrill shout, he commanded them to stop. He recounted the fallout from their reckless actions, highlighting the havoc they had sown, the trauma inflicted upon innocent mortals. Then he told them the news they were yet to hear - how Cypress, once their tenuous link to the mortal realm, had erased his memory of them, severing their vital connection.

"If Paimon could do that with one scarf," he hissed, "how

easy would it be for me to make sure that not one person remembered you? That every book mentioning the names of Beelzebub and Belphegor burns to cinders at my feet, and every trace of you is lost from this side of the veil?"

The brothers dropped their boisterous act that same second and began nervously trying to reason with the Emperor, assuring him and themselves that he would never do such a thing to them. "Your Grace is far too merciful to banish us to obscurity and let us die," said Beelzebub, his statement sounding more like a question, the implicit *"...right?"* remaining unspoken.

Lucifer, shorter than both of the Princes and a third of the width of Belphegor, advanced towards them slowly, his movements predatory and calculated, like a stalking cheetah. The brothers, despite their imposing size and power, backed away nervously, each reaching for the other's hand.

"I am merciful towards *all* in my charge, Prince Beelzebub. That includes King Paimon, whom you've openly and disastrously defied. It includes the subordinate demons who are endangering themselves and the rest of us because you *gormless cretins* led by the worst possible example. And in many ways, it includes everyone who lives on this side of the veil too. *If sacrificing two imbeciles works out for the greater good, I am more than prepared to do so.*"

Belphegor shook his head, intent on calling the Lightbringer's bluff. "You can't do that," he started, but Beelzebub released his hand and punched him hard in his beefy arm before he could continue and dig their quickly expanding hole any deeper.

"Enough, Belph. I don't want to find out whether he can, or whether he will," he muttered, and taking his brother's hand once more, he led him towards the light. Lucifer enveloped them in a radiant glow, and with a gesture most unbecoming of a god of light, sealed the passage behind them.

Two down, and anyone's guess how many more to go.

As the livid Emperor flitted back and forth through the veil, tracking down rogue demons and banishing them back to the side on which they belonged, one man was determined to stay well out of his way. King Belial, all too aware of his role in the mayhem that had unfolded, had sequestered himself within the lush green confines of his office. The blinds were rolled down tight in a futile attempt to create a sense of security, as if the flimsy fabric would have any hope of keeping the Lightbringer out should he choose to appear.

As a king of nature, Belial was used to the slow, steady, strumming rhythm of the earth, not the sudden, violent upheavals that had now become the norm. He could feel the disturbance in the natural order as clearly as if his own fingers had traced the fraying edges of the veil that both separated two worlds and, in some way, held them together.

Alone in the dim light, Belial's thoughts churned as he wrestled with the thought of the long-term consequences of their actions. The delicate ecosystems he'd tended with such care were in the gravest of danger, no longer solely because of human activity but from the fallout of his own kind's recklessness. The forests he loved, the creatures he protected, all were at risk. The fires fueled by the changes in the atmosphere were one threat, but the instability caused by rogue demons was another beast entirely.

As he sat in his chair surrounded by his green wards, hands absentmindedly tracing the carvings in the wood, he felt a gnawing unease. He was the steward of the earth, a protector of its cycles and secrets, yet here he was, hiding like a common criminal with no idea how to shelter it from harm. Before he could dwell on it any further, the piercing ring of the phone on his desk snatched his attention.

Picking up the handset with a cautious *"Hello?"*, he half-expected Lucifer to burst out of the speaker, threatening to let him burn along with his trees for his part in the maelstrom outside.

What he didn't expect was the husky drawl of Armand Devas, or rather, King Asmodeus.

"Something is wrong, Belial," he stated simply.

"What's going on? This isn't a great time, honestly," replied Belial, his voice quiet, seemingly worn out.

"A woman just *slapped me* for trying to get with her."

Belial groaned. "This is why you call me, warning me that something is wrong? What, you want me to be your wingman? Kiss your cheek better? You know, Asmodeus, it was about time someone put you in your place. Good for her."

"You misunderstand me," said Asmodeus. "She wasn't

interested. Which means my abilities are failing me. I hit the blackjack table after, just to convince myself it wasn't true. I'm down ten-kay, Belial. And before you say that's spare change to me, I know that. But with no power of seduction and no unbeatable luck in gambling... who am I? What's happening to me?"

It was the first time Belial had heard true fear in his old friend's voice. Asmodeus, an infernal king who reveled in the sway of chance and the carnal indulgences of humankind, was not one to easily succumb to terror. His realm was one of heady indulgence and thrilling risk, where the outcomes of dice rolls and the ecstasy of forbidden pleasures intertwined in a delicate dance. Gamblers, those poor souls, especially those with one foot already dipped in the dark waters of the occult, had for centuries whispered his name, leaving offerings in shadowed corners of candle-lit rooms, hoping to win his favor. And when Asmodeus smiled upon them, luck inevitably seemed to do the same, unfurling its wings and landing squarely in their laps, transforming the clatter of dice into the tinkling music of serendipity.

The aura of Asmodeus had been palpable even in the most mundane of places for as long as those places had stood. The scent of his power lingered in the smoky haze of poker rooms and the hushed anticipation of lottery draws. He was the spark of adrenaline in the veins of those who flirted with fate, the whispered promise of victory that kept them coming back, hand over hand, to the brink of ruin and rapture.

And his domain extended beyond the gaming tables and betting slips. Asmodeus was also a master of desire, a connoisseur of the carnal whose reputation seemed to be etched into the very building blocks of history. His name had been invoked in tantric rituals and orgies for as long as humans had dared to utter it, his presence a sigh of ecstasy in the ears of lovers seeking transcendence through pleasure.

His sexual exploits were legendary, stories told in breathless whispers and fevered gasps. There were tales of nights where time itself seemed to stop, where even the most pious lost themselves in a labyrinth of sensuality and emerged changed, bearing the mark of his touch. The king had woven himself into the very essence of human desire, a shadowy thread that could never be fully unraveled.

Yet now, that same patron of indulgence and chance knew that he himself stood on the precipice of something unknown and deeply unsettling. Anxiety, unfamiliar and overwhelming, left a discordant note in his voice, jarring against the confidence and control that usually defined him. Belial could feel the weight of it from the other side of the phone, the gravity of the situation picking at the stitches of his own composure. It was as if the dice had been cast into the air, spinning, falling in slow motion, and this time, not even Asmodeus could predict where they might land.

In the dim light of his office, amidst whispering leaves and the hum of unseen insects, Belial's resolve hardened. He had always been a creature of slow, deliberate action, and had initially been on board with the plan to continue living in the mortal world, trying to change it from the inside. But now, the time for patience was well and truly over. He knew the time had come to step beyond the green cocoon of his sanctuary and confront the chaos head-on. The dread in Asmodeus' voice was a warning, a sign that even the most powerful among them were not immune to the consequences of the world's decline.

And Belial knew one thing for sure - he would not wait for the storm to break over them. He would meet it, shape it, and, if necessary, tame it.

CHAPTER FOURTEEN

Belial rose from his desk, his mind set firmly on the long and winding path ahead. He knew that while he ultimately held dominion over that which was needed, the whole plan hinged on the support of Emperor Lucifer. And there was only one person who was sure to be able to sway him. He needed Paimon.

Walking out of his office, Belial swept down the hallway, opening smaller office doors one by one. The faint hum of computers and low chatter spilled from each one, eyes darting up to look at him, but he paid them no mind. At last, he reached a door near the end of the corridor and pushed it open. There, an eyeful of pink told him that he'd found his intern. She was dressed in a lace dress adorned with delicate strawberry motifs, paired with red sneakers boasting pink platform soles, which were perched casually on the desk.

Camilla was sipping an iced coffee, her pastel pink metal cup glinting under the fluorescent lights. She swirled the ice around, the clinking sound punctuating the otherwise quiet room. As the cool liquid touched her lips, she sighed contentedly, savoring the blend of caffeine and caramel. Her eyes were momentarily closed, lost in the simple pleasure of the drink.

When she opened them and saw her boss standing in the doorway, her heart stopped. Startled, she scrambled backward, her sneakers thudding against the floor as she hastily removed them from the desk. The cup wobbled in her shaking hand, ice rattling inside as she tried to steady it. She sat upright, her cheeks flushing a soft pink to match her hair.

"I was just having a break," she gasped, her voice shaky and defensive.

Mr. Bellisle regarded her with a calm gaze - Camilla's minor transgression of office decorum was the least of his concerns. He had far bigger fish to fry.

"I don't care," he shrugged. "As long as your work is done, I am completely unbothered as to how and when you do it. What I do appreciate is that you do as I ask you, when I ask you, so on that note, would you find me Bill and send him to my office?"

"Bill... Anderson?" she asked quietly, swallowing hard.

"To my knowledge, there isn't another Bill here," he told her. "He wouldn't dare say boo to you, Miss Jenkins, don't be frightened of him. Tell him I request - no, that I *demand* - his presence in my office as soon as possible. There's a high chance *he'll* be frightened of *you*, then."

Camilla, unwilling to risk making Bellisle reconsider his decision to overlook her earlier indiscretion, scurried past him and set out to find Bill, trying to ignore the sickly feeling in the pit of her stomach. Thankfully, finding him was as uneventful as Bellisle had promised, and no sooner had they crossed paths than he was off, making a beeline for the elevators.

Minutes later, he arrived at Belial's office door. "Pinkie Pop interrupted my lunch break," he declared in discontent. "You sent for me?"

Belial turned to face him, his expression a strange mix of irritation and relief.

"First of all, you're lucky the Emperor didn't send you back to the other side too, after everything you've been doing," Belial said.

Andras shifted uncomfortably, his eyes flicking to the floor before meeting Belial's gaze. "I know. He did show up, and was none too happy about me siding with Beelz and Belph. But he gave me a second chance on account of me handling the situation with Cypress' friends," he admitted. Then, his tone edged with defensiveness, he added his swipe - "You know. The situation *you* had a big hand in causing."

Belial did not respond beyond a nod, though his stern expression remained. He began pacing the room, running his hands across his head, trying to find the words. "I have a plan," he said finally, and his voice only grew more animated as he continued detailing it. Soon, he spoke with a passion that seemed to electrify the air around him, his steps tracing a path back and forth across the room. Andras' head followed his movements, eyes locked onto Belial as he tried to grasp the weight of what was being said.

When he'd finished. Andras let out a loud hoot of laughter.

"I'll tell you what, King Bee, I'm proud. That is batshit insane. More so than anything I could ever come up with. But I like batshit insane, so count me in. What do you need from me?"

"Right now, I just need you to go to Paimon's stall and bring them here. Tell them their presence is *required*, not requested. It's urgent," Belial instructed.

Andras nodded, a glint of curiosity and mischief in his eyes. "You got it Bel," he called on his way out of the door, Belial muttering a few expletives under his breath in response as Andras made his way to the bustling street below, heading for Paimon's corner in Times Square. The clusters of people he passed by barely noticed him, their lives continuing in blissful ignorance. Ignorance, that is, of both the supernatural dealings happening in their midst and the fact that the city's notorious serial killer was beetling between them, the very hands that had committed those most heinous of crimes nudging them out of the way and patting their shoulders in apology.

As Andras faded into the crowd, Belial walked away from the window and back down the corridor, to the office where he earlier found Camilla. She jumped, her sleek phone in its glittering pink case clattering to the ground. "You'll give me a heart attack one of these days," she panted, but her boss simply smiled back at her, his expression oddly serene.

"I do hope not," he said softly, leaning against the doorway. "I just wanted to give you some advice." She braced herself for a lecture about work etiquette, baffled at what came in its place. "If there was ever a time when you couldn't go to a salon in the same way, or buy chemicals to bleach and color your hair, there's a way to do it naturally. Remember this, Camilla, it may come in handy one day: if you mix lemon juice with chamomile tea and sit in the sun for an hour, it'll lighten your hair right up. Then beets make a charming pink color; you can add avocado skins and pits, dried and ground up, if you want more of a peachy tone. I know... people... who swear by it for dyeing their clothes. Now, it wouldn't look exactly the same, but at least you wouldn't have to be without it. You should always be able to be authentically, unapologetically you. It's what I like about you."

Camilla laughed, unsure what else to do, but instinctively made a mental note of his words anyway. "With all due respect, Mr. Bellisle, you're real weird sometimes," she told him, drawing a laugh from his lips too.

"I know," he called on his way back up the corridor to his own office. "All the best of us are."

A few blocks away, Paimon was closing up their stall, the remnants of another day packed away with care. They looked up as Andras approached, their expression unreadable.

"I'm afraid I'm done for the day, sweetpea, you're gonna have to come back tomorrow," they said, tying the last of the drapes around the stall.

"Don't sweetpea me," Andras huffed. "Anyway, I don't want any of your shiny, silky nonsense. I'm here for you."

Paimon raised an eyebrow, meeting his eye for the first

time. "I'm *enormously* flattered, but you're just not my type, Mr. Anderson," they retorted, flipping their hair over their shoulder dramatically as Andras' jaw clenched visibly tighter.

"You're a-" he began, a number of obscenities on the tip of his tongue, but he stopped himself before letting any of them spill, settling for *"insufferable. You're insufferable."*

"Why, thank you, dearie, the flattery just keeps coming!" Paimon twittered, Andras choosing to ignore their latest attempt at provocation. "What do you want from me, then, if it's not my body?"

Your body would be a great pleasure, but not in the way you're implying.

Andras' minuscule shred of self-control managed to restrain him from saying those words out loud, and so Paimon chose not to acknowledge them.

"Mr. Bellisle sent me to ask you to join him in his office. He told me that your presence is - how did he put it? - *required, not requested.*"

Paimon complied without question, turning to walk with Andras. As they walked together, Paimon glanced at Andras' steely expression, wondering what could be so urgent that Belial would send for them personally.

Before they could put too much thought into it, a familiar face in the crowd drew their attention. They veered towards him, ignoring Andras' vexed grumbles, and were met with a smile.

"Gorgeous art you've got there, sweetie," they grinned, taking in the contents of the large box the man carried around his neck. Small canvas boards with impressionist lakes and birds, hand-painted magnets featuring city landmarks, and notebooks decorated with depictions of unique leaves, impossible vines and rare flowers that seemed strikingly familiar, each adorned with a small white sticker with a handwritten price. "You painted all of those yourself?"

"Yup," the artist responded proudly in a thick Southern accent, shuffling the items around to show the eccentrically dressed person in front of him more. "I sell the bigger pieces at art fairs and things, but I'm saving up some money now to move out of town. So I'm spending my nights making and my days selling. I was just about to head home, so if you wanna give me my last sale of the evening…"

Paimon smiled fondly, plucking three canvases out of the box, each bearing a sticker with $25 scrawled on it. "You're underselling your skills here, honey," they tutted, pulling out a bundle of bills from the depths of their flamboyant sunset-hued robe. They handed it over to the man, who stared at the money in bewilderment.

"What is… I can't accept this, ma'am. Sir? Sorry. Uh…"

"Just call me Taina. Tai is fine, too. And I insist that you take the money; you know, I have a… a large property, in the desert. These paintings will decorate the walls perfectly, and I hope I'll get to snap up some of your bigger pieces too, before you leave."

The artist leafed through the money, trying to count in his head before putting it into his pocket, still thanking his customer profusely, cautious of the city's well-known pickpockets and thieves.

"I'm Cypress, by the way," he said, extending a hand to the person he now once more knew as Tai, who shook it graciously. "I can write down my number so that we can be in touch about the bigger paintings... given how generous you were today, I'm happy to paint something for you at no extra charge."

"Poppycock, darling, you'll be paid for your work, as you should be," they replied. "And don't worry about the number. I'll be in touch."

Cypress narrowed his eyes - from the moment they'd said their name, something had stirred in him, and the feeling of recognition was still niggling in the back of his mind. "Have we met before?" he asked. "I feel like I know you, somehow."

"I have a stall on the streets too," shrugged Paimon. "I probably sold you a jacket, or a scarf, or your mama a dress. It's hard to keep track, I'm sure you understand."

"The green scarf!" nodded Cypress, snapping his fingers. "That's it. It's beautiful, thanks again for that, Tai."

"Well then," smiled Paimon. "As you might say, *I best get to gettin'*."

Cypress smiled and waved, thanking Tai once again, then allowed his hand to slip into his pocket, fondling the thick wad of cash. He still couldn't shake the feeling that something was off about the interaction. *Why were they so generous? How did they remember the way he said goodbye, part of the legacy of his late grandpa, if they couldn't keep track of their customers? Who was the man in the wine-red polo shirt behind them, glaring at them the entire time?* But a stronger feeling yet told him to swallow those questions and go home. And so he did.

Meanwhile, Paimon arrived at Bellisle Media Ltd., entering the CEO's office for the first time. They looked around, awestruck by the lush greenery, the vibrant sense of life that filled the room. It all seemed so... *Belial.* The man himself stood in the center, his presence commanding and composed, yet tinged with a palpable tension.

"Thank you for coming, Paimon," Belial began, his voice smooth and regal, having abandoned any pretense of corporeality. "You know as well as I do that we're facing a crisis. The world is waning, taking not only the mortal creatures but many of our kind with it. We need to act drastically, and we need to do it quickly."

Paimon nodded, their eyes sharp with understanding. "What do you propose?"

Belial gestured to the vibrant foliage surrounding them. "The Fae. My folk, like myself, don't need human belief to survive. No matter how shaky things get with the human world, their power will not be affected. And their moral compasses are more like roulette wheels, so they will do what is required, not simply what is good, or what is asked. I want to leverage that autonomy to stabilize both sides of the veil."

Paimon considered his words carefully. "You want to enlist the Fae to help us? They'll overthrow everything. Nothing will ever be the same."

"Precisely," Belial confirmed. "So I need your support. This mission will change everything. If we succeed, we can restore balance in a way that can never be undone. If we fail… well. The consequences could be catastrophic."

Paimon placed the three paintings they held in their hands down on Belial's desk, briefly tracing the lines of the painted birds before looking back at Belial, recognizing the determination in his eyes.

"Belial, darling, I understand why you believe this to be the best way forward. I do," Paimon said finally. "But this will not be easy. The Fae are unpredictable, and their loyalty is fickle at best."

"I understand that all too well," Belial assured them. "But I believe I have no other choice. As I said, we must act, and we must act now. All I need from you is to take me to the Emperor. You have a direct line to him in a way that most of us don't. Take me to talk to him, and ensure that he listens. Please."

"Very well."

And so Belial opened the blinds, allowing sunlight to flood the room. They stepped, hands intertwined, into the light before emerging from a similar beam that passed through a deep green stained glass window in Emperor Lucifer's great hall. The hall was encircled by eight sets of nine tall, narrow windows, each a link to one of the seventy-two great demons. Belial's window stood among the other eight infernal kings, with Paimon's next to it, though they both emerged through Belial's portal.

Belial's window was a rich mosaic of green hues, accented with deep russet, depicting a woodland scene where rabbits and foxes played among the tree trunks. Paimon's, in stark contrast, was predominantly yellow with hints of pale pink, portraying an abstract desert landscape with a solitary camel beneath a blazing sun. Belial's gaze lingered on Asmodeus' panel, at the other side of his own. Reds, magentas, and oranges swirled to form the nude curves of a voluptuous female body, cards tumbling around her.

The light from the windows bathed the hall in a kaleidoscope of colors, each one telling a story of the demon it represented in a spectacle that was both awe-inspiring and humbling, a testament to the vast power and history of the veiled realms.

Seemingly having sensed their presence, the Emperor himself strode into the room soon after, emerging from a blinding beam of light passing through the centerpiece of the stained glass patchwork - a huge sun and moon, in every iridescent pastel shade imaginable. His delicately sculpted jawline, grazed by his golden hair, was clenched in exasperation.

"Did you suppose I had no better way to spend my time than being here with you two?" he asked, his cloak flowing behind him as he strode towards them, making Belial feel distinctly underdressed in his linen blazer suit. "If you've so far failed to notice, there is all-out pandemonium on the other side of the veil. I am trying my best to fix it, with no assistance from either of you. I hope you have a *very* good excuse for interrupting me."

"My deepest apologies," said Belial, bowing his head. "I asked King Paimon to ensure me a few moments of your time. I have a plan to save human lives, demon lives, my own dominion - the trees, plants, and woodland creatures. But I won't go ahead without your support."

Lucifer stopped mid-step and uncrossed his arms. "Elaborate," he instructed.

"I intend to involve my own subjects in this crisis," Belial said, and Lucifer raised a brow.

"Do you mean your legions? I rather think we've had quite enough of the lower ranks unveiled already, don't you?" he asked, his voice low but firm.

"Forgive me - no, I have no intention of enlisting my legions. This has gone far past their competencies, and mine, and respectfully, yours too."

Belial heard Paimon draw a sharp breath next to him, anticipating a flash of the Emperor's temper, but to both of their surprise, he remained silent, listening.

"I propose inviting the Fae to help me handle the crisis."

And then, for the third time that day, he laid out the plan, each repetition reinforcing his belief in its necessity. It was more than a strategy. It was the embodiment of his commitment to navigating the complexities of their existence with wisdom and foresight. Belial saw his own certainty as a beacon of hope, illuminating the path forward in the midst of uncertainty; as the words flowed from his lips once more, the clarity of his vision sharpened, and the intricate web of strategies and contingencies became ever more vivid in his mind.

The Lightbringer listened to him intently, allowing him to finish before he spoke.

"Paimon. What do you think of this?"

Paimon avoided the gaze of both Belial and Lucifer, knowing that they had no option but to tell the truth. "The Fae folk are no friends of the Djinn, Your Grace. You are, I assume, well aware of that. We're often thought of as similar - both will grant a man his heart's greatest wish while simultaneously making him regret ever making it, after all, but we see them as… unscrupulous, shall we say, and they certainly have no respect for us. I think that, if we've had problems thus far, involving the Fae could prove to be an irreparable disaster. Personally, I could only in good conscience recommend going ahead with the current plan."

Belial felt his heart sink as he listened to Paimon's words. He'd counted on their support - their close connection to the Emperor as his second in command, and their ability to sway him. Instead, they'd driven a stake through the heart of his idea, ensuring the Lightbringer would never grant his assent to the plan. Belial's soul grew heavy in the knowledge that he would either have to watch his dominion burn or advance with his plan in defiant solitude.

But, then, the Emperor spoke. "Sit," he chirped, gesturing

to a gigantic blue and white crystal table, carved from a geode in Paimon's own kingdom, in the center of the hall. He pointed them to two of the twenty chairs carved from the same material, opposite each other, on each side of the table. With a flick of his wrist, he suddenly held something in his hand - a small, ornately carved pistol with a silvery white maplewood handle and a white gold lock and barrel that almost seemed to glow.

He placed it down slowly in the middle of the table between them, watching their confused looks and exchanged glances. "Russian Roulette," he said. "Whoever wins gets their way. Whoever loses isn't here to object."

"With all due respect, Emperor Lucifer, a gun can't…"

"Can't kill you?" predicted the Emperor. "This one can."

"That can't be-" breathed Paimon, but Lucifer's solemn look told them that it was.

Eleos.

Tales of the weapon in front of them had circulated behind the veil for centuries, whispered among the shadows, yet it was largely considered a myth, even by those whose own names had become the stuff of legend.

It was said to have been crafted by Thanatos himself, the God of death, from the wood of a sacred tree. According to the story - though the name of the deity varied with the teller - one of the old Gods hung from that tree for ten days, seeking an end to his suffering. When he was finally cut down, he was mercifully written out of both legend and history, allowing him to fade away. The metal was that of Goliath's own sword, the very one David used to deliver the fatal blow, symbolizing the conquerability of the seemingly unconquerable.

Any bullet fired towards oneself from the barrel of Eleos was destined to fulfill its grim purpose. That, after all, was its sole design; to ensure that should an immortal entity ever be desperate enough to call upon the mercy of Thanatos, he could bestow it upon them.

How the Emperor had ended up in possession of the legendary weapon, neither demon knew. But both stared at it, feeling more vulnerable than they ever had before, in their thousands of years of existence. Their eyes flitted from the gun to each other, daring the occasional brief glimpse at Lucifer, who now sat on his crystal throne at the head of the table, watching silently. Then, Belial's hand whipped forward, grabbing the gun. He pressed the barrel to his still-shaven head, suddenly bleakly aware that he sat before King Paimon and Emperor Lucifer as Matt Bellisle, wishing that if these were his last moments, he'd at least had the presence of mind to die with his true face.

He closed his eyes and pressed the trigger. He braced himself for the crack of the gunshot, but it never came. Instead, he felt a fine dust trickling over his hand. Opening his eyes, he saw that the weapon had disintegrated into a pile of white sand on the floor beside his chair.

"It wasn't..."

"The real one?" Lucifer interjected. "No. I do have it, or rather, the Empress does. Thanatos entrusted it to us for safekeeping, to be used only when absolutely necessary, which I sincerely hope will be never. But I would never use it for such a purpose, nor permit either of you to gamble your lives away."

"I wouldn't have given my life on a gamble anyway, you know that," Paimon cut in. Lucifer turned to face them, acknowledging their statement with a nod.

"I do. And that is how I made my decision."

Paimon and Belial exchanged a glance and then looked back at the Emperor, waiting for him to continue.

"King Belial was willing to sacrifice his life for his cause. He believes so strongly in this plan, and in the ability of the Fae folk to restore balance on the other side of the veil, that he was prepared to make the ultimate sacrifice."

Lucifer approached Belial slowly, taking his hand and bowing his head to plant a feather-light kiss on it.

Belial felt a mix of relief and anticipation. This was it, the turning point, the moment when all his efforts and sacrifices might finally lead to the salvation he sought for both worlds.

"You have my blessing, Belial. May the winds of fate be at your back."

CHAPTER FIFTEEN

In steadfast confidence that the winds of fate indeed howled behind him, Belial wasted no time in setting his plan into motion.

At the fall of night, the king left behind the harsh, modern world for the ancient, eternal beauty of the Fae realm for the first time in too long. His kingdom was a place unravaged by time, where the air was fragrant with the scent of blooming flowers and the songs of birds filled the sky. The ground beneath his feet was soft with moss and delicate ferns, forming a plush carpet that carried him deeper into his domain.

King Belial looked down at his hands, reveling in the now rare opportunity to embrace his true self. His skin was the rich, glistening green of a hydrangea leaf, while his eyes and chest-length hair embodied the soft white of its blooms, giving him a striking spectral appearance. Upon his head rested his great crown, a living diadem of intertwined stems and vines, sprouting leaves and tiny flowers that seemed to bloom just for him.

He surveyed his surroundings with pride that threatened to burst from his chest - the Fae realm was a marvel of natural splendor, with towering trees whose canopies seemed to brush the heavens and crystal-clear streams that wound their way through lush meadows. His palaces and courtyards, constructed from living wood and stone, harmonized with the landscape, their walls adorned with intricate carvings and vibrant flora. This was a place where magic was woven into the very fabric of existence, a testament to the power and beauty of nature, and as he took it in, he was all the more determined to reclaim and rescue the terrains he'd crafted in its image.

As Belial moved through his kingdom, the Fae folk gathered, their attention drawn by the rare presence of their king. They emerged from the shadows of the trees and the depths of the rivers, their forms as varied as the natural world itself. Some were the delicate figures that human children read about in books, with gossamer dresses and wings like dragonflies; others were robust and earthy, their skin resembling bark and their wide eyes gleaming like polished stones. They all shared a deep connection to the land, their lifeblood intertwined with the magic that pulsed through it.

Belial made his way to his glade, a place he had used to hold court for as long as space and time had existed. The glade was framed by towering trees with trunks wrapped in thick moss, their ancient branches reaching out as if to link arms with each other. Beneath the canopy, a vibrant array of rhododendron bushes in every shade of orange and yellow burst into bloom, their petals a rich, warm celebration of life. The whole place was alive with color and light, the sun filtering through the leaves to create dappled patterns on the forest floor. Here, nature's artistry was at its most exuberant, and in the center stood the masterpiece - Belial's throne. It was a magnificent structure crafted for him by his subjects from living branches and vines, and as he approached, it seemed to respond to his presence, the branches twisting and shifting to form a seat fit for a king. He ascended with a noble grace, his presence silencing the murmurs of the assembled Fae folk as he took his place.

The atmosphere was electric with anticipation. The Fae had long been disconnected from the human world in which they knew their King now resided, their influence waning as humanity turned away from nature and embraced the cold, unyielding advance of materialism. They knew that Belial had summoned them for a purpose, and he knew that whatever he said now would change the course of both their world and that on the other side of the veil forever.

As he prepared to reveal his plan, the Fae watched him in reverence and curiosity. In the silence that swirled around them, the only sound was the soft rustle of leaves and the distant chirping of tits and finches in the trees overhead. Belial took a deep breath, drawing in the life and magic of his realm, and began to speak.

He rose from his throne, surveying the assembly of Fae with a calm but commanding presence. His blossom-white eyes swept over the gathered faces, each one living, breathing proof of the primordial magic weaved throughout every aspect of the natural world. Even the glade itself, bathed in the golden light of dawn filtering through the moss-draped branches, seemed to hold its breath in suspense.

"My beloved ones," he began, his regal power resonating in his voice. "We stand at a pivotal moment in the history of two realms. The mortal world, once so intertwined with the magic and harmony of nature, is now lost in the darkness of its own shadows. Obsessions with technology and money have consumed human society, driving a wedge between them and the natural world."

He paused, giving his words a moment to sink in, his gaze steady and unyielding. Long ago, they had lived in relative harmony with the humans, guiding and nurturing their growth, ensuring a balance between their ambitions and the world around them. But as the human world grew more independent and less spiritual, their material desires more insatiable, a separation occurred. The Fae withdrew, retreating behind the veil to preserve their essence and watch from afar. It had led to a sense of resentment among many of his subjects, and he was aware that that resentment may be the deciding factor in how they received his words.

Belial's voice softened as he recounted the past, a muted tint of sorrow coloring his words. "There was a time when our presence was felt in every forest, every wood, every field. When humanity revered the trees, the fruits, the very earth beneath their feet. But now, their world is consumed by concrete and steel."

He took a deep breath before continuing, the air seeming to thicken with the intensity of his speech. "The greatest threat to their side of the veil - and therefore our side too - is their blind, passive belief that something must be done. *They* have to do this, *they* have to stop that. Always *they*, never *we*.

And that is why we can no longer allow them to be both marble and sculptor; *they are hacking away mindlessly with a chisel they refuse to see they wield."*

His vision was clear and unfaltering; he was ready to fight for a future where nature reigned supreme, where the Fae would lead humanity back to a life in harmony with the earth. "This is not a call for destruction," he warned, "but for reclamation. We will show them the beauty of the world they have abandoned, and in doing so, we will save them from themselves."

The assembly fell uncannily silent, each Fae contemplating the words of their monarch. Slowly, the glade began to fill with murmurs and whispers, until finally, someone spoke aloud.

"Your Majesty," called an old wood nymph with limbs like twisted branches and pale lilac hair like drooping wisteria flowers hanging to her waist. "This plan could pose untold dangers to my people, to all of us. The technology they've developed… can't it be used against us?"

King Belial walked down the steps of his throne, standing directly in front of her.

"My dear Acanthacea," he said, placing a strong hand on her scrawny, ligneous shoulder. "You and I have known each other for many more years than humans have walked the Earth. I sincerely hope that you know I would never allow you, your people, or any of the Fae folk to risk their lives in this attack. We will overthrow the tyranny of materials, sprouting plants and trees where lifeless buildings and machines now stand.

It will be difficult, but in the end, humanity will remember the magic they have lost."

More questions and concerns were tossed from the crowd, but the King was prepared - he addressed his people coolly and calmly, reassuring them one by one. His presence was a beacon of hope, and his plan a lifeline for two worlds on the brink of collapse. "There is no more time to waste. We will move at dawn," he declared after the crowd once again fell silent, his voice ringing with finality. "Together, we will reclaim nature's place in the world and restore the balance that has been lost. For the sake of all living things, we come together, and we act as one."

With that, Belial sat back on his throne, the lush green of his skin blending seamlessly with the foliage around him.

This time, his words were met by raucous applause. The glade erupted into a symphony of sound, a chorus of approval and ancient battle cries that echoed through the woodland. The Fae came together as one, celebrating the declaration of their king with fervor: the wood nymphs, their bodies slender and bark-like, raised their branchesque arms to the sky, chanting in a tongue as old as the trees they guarded. The leaves on the rhododendron bushes around them quivered in response as if nature itself was joining their exultation.

The sylphs took to the air, their fragile wings glittering in the dappled sunlight. They spun and twirled above the assembly, their laughter like the tinkling of wind chimes. With every swoop, they created miniature whirlwinds that scattered petals and leaves in a colorful shower, falling around the monarch like confetti.

The naiads, with their hair flowing like streams and ocean-blue eyes, added their voices to the rising tide of elation. They sang ancient war songs, melodies that rushed and rolled like white water rivers as the trickling brook that wound through the glade seemed to swell in response, its waters sparkling more brightly in the glow of its guardians.

At the edge of the mob stood the mossgoblins and rocksprites, smaller but by no means less fierce than the rest of the beings in the glade. Their faces were alight with mischief and determination, their cheers sharp and staccato. They brandished tiny weapons made from sharpened stones and twigs, their cries reminiscent of long-forgotten clashes between each other, fought in defense of their hidden caves and groves.

As the cheers, chants, and applause swelled to a crescendo, Belial felt a surge of pride and determination. The Fae folk were united, ready to follow him into the human world and reclaim the harmony that had been lost. His vision was no longer just his own; it was shared by every being in his kingdom, each one ready to fight not for him, but for a future where nature reigned supreme across realms.

Belial raised a large, tapered hand, and while the noise gradually subsided, the air still buzzed with anticipation and the unspoken promise of action. Dawn would bring a new beginning, a chance to restore the world to its natural state and guide humanity back to the path they had strayed from. The Fae dispersed, making plans and preparations, but the king himself remained seated for a while, the weight of his decision now heavy upon his shoulders.

When he finally rose, he wandered inchmeal through his kingdom, the viridian beauty of the realm offering both solace and a stark reminder of what was at stake.

He moved silently through woodlands adorned with wildflowers in every shade imaginable, their vibrant blooms sleeping softly in the moonlight. Prehistoric trees, their gargantuan trunks cloaked in moss and mushrooms, loomed above him, their leaves in the night breeze seeming to whisper secrets of old. Streams of silvery water wound their way through the landscape, their gentle babble a soothing antithesis to the turmoil in Belial's mind.

As the night wore on, the sleepless sovereign found himself drawn to a secluded clearing, a place of personal reflection where he had come countless times over countless years to think. He sat beneath a towering monkeypod tree, its branches spreading protectively above him, and placed his crown at his side. The leaves that bowed to take its place around his head rustled softly, a lullaby from nature itself, but sleep nonetheless eluded him. His mind raced with the enormity of what lay ahead - the inevitable clash of realms, the overthrow of human obsessions, and the return of the world to its natural state.

The silence of the night was profound, broken only by the occasional calls of nocturnal creatures. Belial's thoughts, left uninterrupted, turned to a reluctant Paimon, a chaos-hungry Andras, and the other allies who would undoubtedly play crucial roles in the coming upheaval. He knew the path they were embarking upon was fraught with danger and uncertainty, but he refused to allow himself to harbor doubt - it was also right, and just, and above all, *necessary*.

As the hours passed, the inky darkness of the sky began to lighten, the first hints of daybreak creeping over the horizon. Belial rose from his contemplative spot and returned his crown to its place atop his thick cloud-white hair, his heart heavy, but his will unyielding. He wandered back towards his palace, the luxuriant colors of the Fae realm becoming more pronounced with each step as the night gave way to day.

Finally, he reached his garden and stood looking outwards, surrounded by its towering ferns and delicate bellflowers that swayed in the gentle morning breeze. He watched as the first light of dawn broke over his realm, the sun's rays flooding through the canopy, casting an Elysian glow over everything they touched. It was a new dawn, not just for the Fae, but for the world beyond the veil, and King Belial stood still, absorbing it. The light of dawn bathed him in its warmth, a symbol of the renewal and change that was to come.

And as a kingdom awoke around its king, he felt his ambition rise with it.

The time had come.

CHAPTER SIXTEEN

The first sign was subtle: phones across the world began to flicker, their screens going dark. A momentary glitch, some thought, before resuming their morning rituals.

But the glitches didn't stop. And by mid-morning in New York, the city King Belial had called home, panic had set in. As was happening everywhere, communication systems failed. In office buildings, the flickering of monitors and the static on teleconference screens grew more frequent, until finally, they went dark altogether.

The once-reliable subway networks that connected the sprawling metropolis sputtered and died; commuters stood in the stations, staring in confusion at the blackened boards that usually listed train schedules. Buses idled at stops as their drivers wondered why their automated systems were down, unable to reach the depot via radio.

Even in Times Square, the colossal digital billboards flickered and buzzed loudly before going blank, leaving an eerie void where vibrant advertisements once dominated the backdrop of daily life. The absence of the usual bombardment of colors and sounds was disconcerting, an unsettling visual silence.

In homes, the fear was even more palpable. Parents tried in vain to reach schools to check on their children, their calls met with nothing but a deafening silence. Teens, accustomed to the constant chatter of social media, found themselves disconnected from their partners and friends in unprecedented solitude, their screens stubbornly refusing to display the familiar feeds. Emergency services struggled to respond to the crisis, their dispatch systems paralyzed.

Throughout the day, it progressed - television screens worldwide turned to static, and radio stations played only silence. The airwaves, once filled with music, news, and chatter, were void. In cities everywhere, people emerged from their homes, drawn by the collective unease. They gathered in clusters on street corners, in parks, and outside buildings, their faces masks of confusion and fear.

The collective alarm continued to spread as rumors began to circulate, each more outlandish than the last, and yet none coming close to the inconceivable truth. Some whispered of a Russian cyber-attack or the revenge of a nameless group of hackers, while others speculated about government cover-ups. Conspiracy theories blossomed, feeding on the fear and uncertainty that gripped the world.

Amidst the chaos, the Fae moved unseen, their phantasmic forms weaving effortlessly through the fabric of the mortal world. But their presence, though not seen, was felt - in the growing unease and the subtle shifts in the natural world, people found the realization that something beyond their wildest imaginations may be afoot. Plants began to sprout in the most unlikely places - ferns unfurling on train tracks, vines creeping over concrete barriers and winding around streetlights, and spunky little coneflowers bursting from the cracks of the asphalt.

King Belial watched on from his office, using his vantage point while he still could, his heart swelling with satisfaction. As he had hoped, the first attack was not one of violence, but of reclamation.

The Fae's magic had already disrupted the technological web that had ensnared humanity, forcing people to look up from their screens and face the world around them. Even in the confusion, there was a strange, almost poetic beauty. For the first time in a long while, people were talking to each other, sharing their fears, and seeking comfort in the presence of their fellow humans.

Around the world, a new level of disarray unfolded as bank buildings mysteriously burned to the ground overnight. In city after city, the financial fortresses that once epitomized stability and power were reduced to smoldering ruins. There were few witnesses, but those who laid eyes upon the fires spoke in hushed tones about the strange events they'd observed; they swore they saw the smoke rise and twist into the shape of a sigil - a disturbing form that looked like *"a skull, or perhaps a tower."*

With digital cameras and smartphones now eerily inert, capturing the otherworldly displays became a near-impossible task. The few who possessed old film cameras scrambled to document the strange occurrences, but by the time they returned, the smoke had settled into a simple billowing pillar reaching into the sky. The lack of evidence only fueled the fires of speculation and fear, as people grappled with the inexplicable events that had shattered the illusion of modern security and control.

As the ashes of once-imposing bank buildings settled, so too did a sense of foreboding, the world left to ponder what unseen forces were now operating.

And as time marched on, it became abundantly clear that the vice grips of technology and money would not be released quite as easily as Belial and the Fae folk had hoped. By the end of the first week of the blackout, the city - like many others around the globe - had descended into utter havoc. With no means to communicate, no way to access bank accounts or pay for basic necessities, and no idea what was going on, the thin veneer of civilized society began to fray and tear.

The streets, once ticking along in an orderly sort of chaos, now thrashed with a more desperate energy. Supermarkets were ransacked as people fought over dwindling supplies. Without electronic transactions, and with the burnings of banks around the world leaving its citizens without a way to access cash, bartering quickly became the new currency, with canned goods and bottled water traded for other essentials.

The parking lot outside one looted supermarket had become a makeshift marketplace of desperation. Among overturned shopping carts and discarded debris, two figures stood face to face, their voices strained with urgency.

A young woman with wild, unkempt hair and tear-streaked cheeks clutched a bundle of canned goods to her chest. Across from her stood a burly man with rough hands and a scowl etched deeply into his weathered face. In a shopping basket between them lay a meager pile of goods: a half-empty bottle of water, a loaf of bread, and a handful of tinned vegetables.

"You ain't got nothin' I need, lady!"

The man's voice was gruff, his eyes darting nervously around the lot. His hand hovered over a rusted knife tucked into his belt.

The woman's grip on her provisions tightened. "Please, Sir. My son, Lucas, he's four. He's sick. He needs water, the shit in our apartment isn't clean. I'll give you all these cans for that water. *Please.*"

His thin lips curled into a sneer. "Thankfully for me, li'l Lucas ain't my problem. You think I care about your brat? I told you, I don't need no damn vegetables, or beefaroni, or whatever else you got there."

The young mother's haggling turned to pleading. "I'll find something else to trade," she whimpered. "*Anything.* Please, just the water."

A tense silence hung between them, broken only by the occasional shout from nearby alleys. The man's gaze flickered towards her trembling hands and the cans of food gripped in them. Without warning, he lunged forward, knocking her to the ground with a forceful shove. The cans spilled across the pavement, rolling away in all directions as she cried out in anguish, scrambling to retrieve the cans before they were lost.

"No! Please!"

The man stooped to snatch the water bottle from the ground, his eyes blazing with a mix of triumph and rage. "You shouldn't have tried me, bitch," he spat before bolting into the darkness.

Her heart pounded in her chest as she backed away, clutching the few cans she managed to salvage. Tears streamed down her face as she watched her assailant retreat into the shadows, the precious water bottle still in his possession. Around her, the other desperate souls in the parking lot exchanged wary glances, their own bartering transactions pausing momentarily at the eruption of violence. In a new world without technology or law enforcement, survival had quickly become a brutal game of chance where compassion and reason were often overshadowed by fear and necessity.

She cradled the cans to her chest, her hands trembling with a mixture of relief for herself and sorrow for her son. She knew she had narrowly escaped a worse fate, but she remained without water, having gained only a deep wound in her already fragile sense of hope.

She was not alone in her sense of helplessness and isolation. It was palpable throughout the city and beyond, and for some, it was too much to bear. The decision to end it all became a distressingly common one, though without the media to broadcast the grim tally, the tragedies went largely unnoticed by the masses. Yet more lives ended involuntarily as medications, life support machines, and mobility aids fell into a grim obsolescence. Each life lost was a silent testament to the overwhelming despair that had taken root in the city.

Family separations, once mitigated by the constant connectivity of the modern age, now became a source of profound anguish, echoing through the devastated streets. Parents wandered the sidewalks with hollow eyes, clutching photos of their children and scanning faces in crowded makeshift shelter centers, hoping for a familiar smile among the sea of strangers.

Siblings, normally a text message away, found themselves separated by miles and circumstance, their only connection now the fading memories of shared laughter and tears.

Lovers, once bound by late-night calls and digital messages, stood on opposite sides of the world, screaming in vain at the sky, their yearning hearts echoing the desperation of those around them.

The exodus from urban centers was swift and chaotic. Streets teemed with people carrying hastily packed bags, their steps faltering under the weight of uncertainty. Every journey was a gamble against time and distance, driven by the primal urge to find safety in the arms of a mother, a father, a child, a spouse. The highways, once symbols of connectivity and progress, became choked with cars packed with strangers, brought together by sharing a destination.

In the suburbs and neighboring towns, makeshift reunions unfolded with bittersweet joy amidst the backdrop of uncertainty. Tearful embraces mingled with whispered apologies and fervent promises never to lose touch again. Strangers opened their doors to weary travelers, offering shelter and solidarity in a world where trust had, almost overnight, become a rare commodity.

While the human world grappled with its new reality, nature continued its quiet, inexorable resurgence, aided from beyond the veil. Delicate shoots pushed through cracks in the pavement, and vines crept up the sides of buildings. Moss continued its unstoppable spread, blanketing sidewalks and climbing up walls with an otherworldly speed as trees burst forth seemingly overnight, their roots breaking through the asphalt and concrete that had once imprisoned them.

The city's famous skyline, once a testament to human ingenuity and dominance over nature, began to look more like a scene from an ancient, forgotten world. The once-proud buildings now bore the marks of nature's reclamation; window sills cradled nests of birds, and ivy wove abstract patterns across glass and steel. The city once known as a concrete jungle was now more akin to a literal one, where flora reigned supreme and fauna roamed freely.

And the Fae watched, still unseen, still picking apart the fabric of the human world.

Their work was far from done, but with the first steps taken, they were confident that their king's plan was unfolding; Belial himself sprouted a tree here and made sure a family woke up in the same place there, but for the most part, he stood back and observed.

He saw his subjects sow a slow and deliberate dismantling of the old order to make way for something new, something more harmonious. He also saw that the human resistance was strong, perhaps even stronger than expected, and the road ahead was fraught with uncertainty.

Yes, the balance was shifting, but it remained to be seen whether the Fae could steer it towards the renewal they envisioned, or if humanity would simply find a way to reclaim its lost dominion.

In the midst of this upheaval, dawn broke over the city, casting a soft light over the transformed landscape. Sixteen blocks from a now desolate Times Square, Cypress Rafferty opened his eyes and glanced towards his window, where green tendrils of ivy were pushing their way through the frame. He walked over and looked out, taking in the scene before him. Leaves, flowers, and fungi were overtaking the once-gray buildings across the street, and grass sprouted defiantly from the cracked pavement below.

It reminds me of something I've seen before.

No, I'd remember seeing a place quite as... green as this.

Perhaps I saw it in a dream.

Shaking the thought from his tousled head, Cypress got dressed, preparing for the long walk down the stairs. The elevator had ground to an unceremonious halt on the very first day of the upheaval, thankfully unoccupied, and Cypress had complained just as much as every other tenant above the third floor. With time, though, he had come to enjoy his daily descents from the twenty-ninth floor to the ground. Each journey was a revelation. He met neighbors he had never known existed, sharing brief, profound moments with them.

And as the plants continued to grow in impossible places, each stairwell and hallway transformed into a garden, bringing with it a menagerie of tiny creatures. Where cockroaches were once the extent of the wildlife, lizards, spiders, dormice, and raccoons now made themselves at home. Cypress liked to think of it as a nature hike on his own doorstep, quickly learning to love the surreal blend of the familiar and the fantastical.

He wandered down slowly, as he always did in recent days, in no rush to reach the bottom. As he reached the seventeenth floor, a large, messy bun of black hair came into view, and he quickly recognized its owner as Dayanara, the fifteen-year-old daughter of the Garcia family.

They'd shared a building for the entire three years that Cypress had lived there, and yet, he'd only recently learned their names - Rita, the mother, was a baker. She'd brought most of the supplies from her little artisan shop home when she'd realized things weren't getting any better, and often left trays of bread outside for her neighbors to help themselves. Domingo, the father, was a loud and proud man who Cypress always privately thought was perhaps too harsh on his family, but for the most part, he seemed to have his heart in the right place. Arbelis, the youngest, was just three. She enjoyed watching the lizards in the hallway, and Cypress had given her some paints to keep herself busy, which meant the white walls outside their door were now splattered with tiny pastel handprints. And Dayanara... well, she was Dayanara. By all accounts, a typical teenager.

"Y'alright there, kiddo?" he asked, reading her hunched posture and the sullenness that seemed to darken the air around her. The girl whipped her head around, looking up at him before rolling her eyes and looking down at the little pink and black charms on her chunky foam clogs again, feigning a laser focus on their doodle-like designs.

Assuming that she was in no mood to answer, Cypress walked carefully around her, continuing his walk down the increasingly overgrown staircase. Then, a voice called after him.

"I'm bored."

He spun on his heel, looking back at his young neighbor. "You're... *bored?*" he asked incredulously. "The whole darn world has gone cattywampus out there, people are dying all over the place, they're saying things might never turn back on... and *you're bored?!*"

"*So* freaking bored," she insisted, her wide brown eyes staring back at him as if she couldn't quite believe that he didn't understand. "I ain't seen one friend since all this happened. Ain't talked to any of them. As soon as my name ain't popping up on their screens, I guess it's out of sight, out of mind. When I'm right there in the little box in their hand, it's fine. But none of those friends really exist, I guess. When there's no phone, there's no them. There's no one. So, yeah - I'm bored shitless."

Cypress smiled sympathetically, unsure what to do or say. "Do you want to come walk with me?" he asked finally. "I'm just gonna go... check it all out. See what the park looks like. Maybe try to find something edible, since I'm almost out of your mom's bread."

Dayanara shook her head, muttering a barely audible

"thanks, though," a declination which Cypress, though he'd never tell, was massively relieved by. He nodded in acknowledgment, wishing her well and continuing down the stairs, deep in contemplation over her words. He'd struggled with not being able to contact his loved ones back home, of course, but he hadn't for a second considered that for some, their entire social network was simply switched off.

When he finally reached the bottom, he paused for a moment as he opened the door to the outside world - he could have sworn it looked even greener than it had yesterday. Stepping out, he felt a soft, squishy sensation beneath his feet in place of the familiar concrete as he stepped onto the grassy moss that was quickly overtaking it in a surreal blend of urban decay and vibrant, unrestrained nature. He watched as small animals, unrecognizable as they moved so fast, darted through the undergrowth that had sprouted around the burnt-out dumpster in the alleyway opposite him, and took a deep breath, the air fresh and filled with the earthy scent of greenery.

Cypress walked on, finding an odd sense of deep-set familiarity in the uncertainty of this new reality, the way it had his senses heightened and his mind alert. The path ahead was unclear, but one thing wasn't: the world was offering him a chance to rediscover it, to find where he belonged in a place reborn from chaos. And he was ready to give it a chance.

CHAPTER SEVENTEEN

As Cypress drifted through the city's veins, he found himself wondering if he'd found himself in another dimension. Trees erupted from cracked sidewalks, their roots lifting slabs of concrete as if they were paper. Once-sterile buildings were now canvases for moss and creeping ivy, weaving together in intricate patterns over brick and steel.

Even the air was alive, humming with the sounds of nature; birdsong replaced the distant hum of traffic, and the rustle of leaves provided their beat like a soft drum announcing the arrival of a world returned to its primeval state. Coyotes darted through alleyways with a newfound boldness, their movements confident and unhurried, as though they had always belonged there - and in some way, Cypress realized, they truly had. Their sleek bodies meandered through the maze of what was once human territory, now a sprawling wilderness in the heart of the city. High above, flitting between the towering buildings now conquered by plants and fungi, birds of all sizes and colors filled the sky with their calls. It was as if the city's soul had been reborn, its essence infused with the untamed beauty of nature.

Cypress's footsteps were muffled by the moss and wildflowers that now carpeted the streets. He stopped to watch in awe as a family of deer grazed in what used to be a bustling intersection, their gentle presence a glaring contrast to the roaring, beeping chaos that once ruled. The scene was almost *too* serene, a perfect tableau of nature's triumph over man.

Then - *BANG*. The sharp crack of gunshot shattered the tranquil atmosphere. As it collapsed, so did one small deer, her graceful legs crumpling beneath her as her family scarpered in panic. Cypress's heart pounded as he saw a man with grim determination etched on his face emerge from the bushes, grab the carcass by its hind legs, and began dragging it away. His initial reaction was anger, a surge of indignation at the violent intrusion into the serenity. But as he watched the man struggle with his burden, he understood the harsh reality: in this new world, hunting wasn't the trophy sport many of his dad's friends back home treated it as. It was a matter of survival. With fast food chains closed and grocery store shelves empty with no hope of restocking, those with the means to hunt had little choice but to use their skills to feed their families.

He felt a leaden sadness settle over him as he accepted this new order, knowing that the sight of the dead deer, a symbol of the old world's destruction and the new world's harsh realities, would become all too normal. He watched the man and the deer disappear completely into the overgrowth before continuing his walk, his steps now a little heavier, each one carrying him further into the great unknown that he had recently called home.

And as he resumed his exploration, he quickly stumbled upon a pocket of life that offered a different kind of hope. He found himself at the edge of a newly sprouted community garden, where the air was filled with the rich scent of earth and growth.

Here, people from all walks of life came together, kneeling in the soil, planting vegetables and herbs, sharing seeds and tools. Cypress watched as a woman handed a trowel to a boy of around five years old, guiding his small hands to dig a hole for a tomato plant, and he smiled. To all who witnessed it, the gesture was a small but powerful sign of resilience, a testament to humanity's ability to adapt and thrive even in the most arduous of adversity. A glimmer of hope that maybe, just maybe, things would turn out okay.

As Cypress looked around at the rest of the faces, one young man in his late teens, with dirt-streaked hands and a smudge of soil on his cheek, looked up from his meticulous rows of cucumber seeds. His face lit up with excitement as he spotted Cypress, and he straightened himself, brushing his hands on his worn jeans.

"Hey there, new guy!" he called out, his voice brimming with enthusiasm. "You won't believe what's happening just around the corner." He paused for dramatic effect, his eyes sparkling with a sense of wonder. "A little market has popped up!"

"Oh, Asher, give it a break, bro," teased his friend, who was still focused on painstakingly sowing tiny seeds. "I thought you were lame for spending every night helping your bubbe in the library, but your obsession with this market is taking it to a new level."

But the young man, apparently named Asher, paid him no mind. He gestured animatedly with his hand, pointing in the direction of the market. "It's so cool," he continued, his words tumbling over each other in his eagerness to share the news. "People have set up these stalls, trading everything from fresh produce to handmade clothes. It's like something out of a different time, you know? No money, just people helping each other out."

"That *does* sound cool," Cypress replied earnestly with a fond laugh. "I'm heading that way anyway; I'll be sure to check it out. Thanks, kid."

He kept his word, and when he got there, he found that Asher was right enough - makeshift stalls lined the street, displaying an array of goods that harkened back to simpler times. Fresh produce, handmade clothing, and simple tools were laid out for trade, and Cypress watched, fascinated, realizing just how much you can tell about a person by the things they need and the things they can spare. An elderly man offered a bundle of carrots in exchange for a rudimentary wooden rake. A young woman traded several small pots of fresh herb plants for a hand-sewn maternity dress. In the absence of money, a new, rudimentary economy was taking shape, based on mutual need and cooperation.

The market buzzed with a different kind of energy than the chaotic frenzy of the stalls that came before it. It was a quieter, more sustainable form of survival.

Children played at the edges of the market, chasing each other around the stalls while their parents bartered and exchanged goods. The sense of community was palpable, and Cypress lingered in it, soaking in the scenes of cooperation and ingenuity. The garden and market were, in his eyes, small beacons at the end of an increasingly dark and dizzying tunnel.

And yet, the darkness was not absent even there.

As he approached what looked like an old school desk laden with vibrant vegetables, Cypress noticed a commotion brewing; two men stood on opposite sides of a particularly large butternut squash, their faces flushed with anger. The larger of the two, a stocky man with a thick beard and a torn flannel shirt, held the squash tightly in his hands. The other, a wiry fellow with sunken cheeks and a ragged cap, was gesticulating wildly, his voice rising above the din of the market.

"I found it first, asshole!" the wiry man shouted, his voice shaking with a mix of desperation and fury. "I've got a family to feed, and this thing could keep us going for days."

The larger man scoffed, tightening his grip on the vegetable. "Newsflash, buddy: everyone here's got a family to feed," he retorted, his tone equally heated. "I've got mouths to fill too, and this beauty's going home with me."

Cypress felt the tension in the air thickening, the surrounding shoppers slowing their activities to watch the unfolding drama. The market's fragile peace was at risk of shattering, all over a single squash.

Then shatter it did: without warning, the wiry man lunged forward, trying to wrestle the squash from the larger man's hands. A struggle ensued, each man refusing to let go. Shouts turned to grunts as they grappled, and Cypress edged closer, hoping to intervene before things got out of hand, but it was too late. The larger of the two men, losing his patience, swung a fist at his opponent, landing a solid punch on the wiry man's jaw. He stumbled back, readjusting his cap which the blow had knocked askew, then retaliated with a right hook of his own that left blood trickling from the other man's lip. The crowd gasped in unison and formed a circle around them, some yelling at the men to stop or trying to pull them apart while others simply watched in stunned silence.

Everyone, including the men themselves, knew it wasn't just about a squash. It was about the uncertainty that gripped everyone, the fear of not knowing where the next meal would come from. It was a stark reminder of how close to the edge they all were, how quickly civility could crumble under the ever-growing weight of their desperation.

Finally, the onlookers managed to separate the men, each being held back by firm hands. The squash lay forgotten on the ground, bruised and battered, having rolled under the table. The market slowly resumed its activity, but the air remained charged with unease.

As Cypress walked away, he couldn't shake the image of the fight from his mind. It was a sobering reminder that while the community was finding ways to adapt, the underlying desperation was never far from the surface. The world had changed, and they were all still trying to find their place in it, one bartered squash at a time. And beyond the boundaries of the mini market, he knew that there were corners of the city where things looked darker yet.

Groups of scavengers, their eyes hollow with desperation and their clothes tattered from the endless search, combed through the remnants of abandoned stores and homes.

These were the people who had nothing left to trade, no goods to barter or produce to cultivate. Their survival depended on whatever they could unearth from the forsaken shells of the world that once was. They moved like wraiths through the night, their footsteps silent and their movements cautious. Each building they entered was a potential treasure trove, holding within its decaying walls the promise of survival - but also a potential encounter with a fellow scavenger, which spelled mortal danger. They sifted through the rubble of what were once vibrant shops and cozy homes, looking for anything that could be of use - canned goods, tools, clothing, even old books that could be used for fuel or, in some cases, for their long-forgotten knowledge.

Looting had become rampant, another telltale sign that the thin veneer of civilization had worn away to reveal a more primal instinct for survival; now, the rule of law was nothing more than a distant memory, a fading echo of a time when order reigned.

As Cypress wandered in deep contemplation, the rhythm of his steps grew slower, then still, as he approached a towering edifice that loomed against the skyline. He already knew this was no ordinary building; it was once the proud home of the country's largest news corporation, a monolith of modern media. Now, it stood silently, like a gravestone; the once-glossy facade was slowly being overtaken by a creeping green blanket. Cypress's gaze was drawn upward to a striking sight: at one of the highest windows, a cascade of growth spilled forth, spilling outwards like a living waterfall. And as he moved closer, the peculiarities of nature's reclamation became even more pronounced; brilliant hues of tropical flora - lush, broad-leafed plants in deep blues and fiery oranges - were entwined with the creeping ivy, their vivid petals catching the light in a dazzling display.

The plants painted a tangled mural of exotic life against the drab backdrop of the building's exterior, their dazzling colors clashing with, and quickly subduing, the grays and silvers of the urban decay. Bright, flowering vines cascaded from the upper windows, their tendrils dancing a tangled twist through the air as they sought new surfaces to cling to.

Curiosity tugged at the pit of Cypress' stomach as he admired the building's transformation. Small, glittering insects, somehow familiar despite being unlike any he had seen before, darted amongst the blossoms. Their wings shimmered with a spectrum of colors, flitting like tiny, living rainbows through the foliage. Among the leaves and blooms, he spotted lizards with scales that glinted metallically in the sunlight. They clambered up the vines with agile ease, their movements as fluid and graceful as the plants they navigated.

He froze for a moment, an indescribable feeling stirring within him.

There's something about this building.

Something that tugged at the edge of his memory, a vague sense of familiarity he couldn't quite place. The sight of that particular window evoked a sense of invitation, as if it were beckoning him to explore what lay within.

Recognition.

That was it - the feeling was recognition. But it was fleeting and elusive, like a half-remembered childhood dream. He assumed it was merely an echo of a film or some other relic of the past, a whisper from a time before the world had so dramatically changed, and walked on, wondering what secrets might be hidden behind those overgrown walls; little did he realize that those secrets were not distant, abstract mysteries but fragments of a story in which he himself had once been a main character.

Unbeknownst to him, just out of earshot, the whispers of the unveiled murmured through the frondescence of the very office that he had once entered and left as a changed man, burdened with truths and revelations that had irrevocably altered the course of his life. His life, and perhaps the world.

But now, he walked on, oblivious to a conflict from another world unfolding within.

King Belial stood in the full blaze of the regality he'd long been forced to dim, his mantle of leaves seamlessly blending into the verdant backdrop of what had once been the office of Matt Bellisle. The wind, carrying the scent of sweet wildflowers and acrid earth, swept through the open window, stirring his white hair into a silken flow. His eyes, with the soft glow of moonlit snow, carefully surveyed the figure standing before him; shorter than Belial, with a build that suggested agility and grace, they stood adorned in vibrant silks and beads that shimmered and danced with every movement. Their silk robes, in hues of deep red, fuschia, and radiant gold, flowed around them like water, while the beads clinked softly, like an echo of ancient music from a distant land.

"Death and destruction were supposed to be avoided, not *caused*," they snapped.

Belial sighed. "I wish it were that simple, Paimon," he said, "but destruction is a vital part of rebirth. And death is the only certain part of life on this side of the veil; for this world to function naturally, death and decay must be allowed to happen naturally."

Paimon glared at him, their eyes dark with resentment. "I understand that, but not like this. Is this really what you envisioned, in the Emperor's hall, is *that out there* what you were willing to give your own life for?"

Belial was silent; Paimon took it first for contemplation, but as they studied his face, a chilling realization seeped in.

"You knew."

When the viridescent king again gave no response, Paimon raised their voice. "You knew, didn't you? You never thought you were risking your life. You never believed that was truly Eleos, admit it!"

"I did, at least for a brief moment," insisted Belial. "When I reached for the gun, I believed it was genuine. When I touched it... Paimon, you know as well as I do that I hold the title of Lord of Lies.

What honor would I bring that title, could I not recognize deception in my own hands?"

When he met Paimon's eyes, they were blazing, the relentless ire of the desert sun within them. "You tricked Emperor Lucifer. You tricked me."

"Of course I did," nodded Belial calmly. "For the good of the world, and everyone and everything in it. You knew my nature when you sat across the table from me, and the Emperor knew it too. Neither of you can blame me for being precisely what I've always been and will always be; rather ask yourself why you didn't expect it."

Paimon turned without another word and left, tearing through the building like a fireball. The redundant light fixtures flickered back to life in a final, convulsive burst of energy as the djinn passed them, erupting into sparks before crashing down. They hung from their wires, swinging erratically in Paimon's wake.

Meanwhile, Cypress, oblivious to having narrowly missed a chance encounter with a familiar face, had wandered into what was once Central Park. Now, the park was more like an antediluvian forest, shrubs and trees claiming every inch of space, transforming the landmark from a tourist magnet to a peaceful place of meditation and contemplation for those seeking calm amidst the chaos. He found a secluded spot among the overgrown greenery and lay down on the soft, cool grass, his mind spinning faster, faster, *faster,* until it was a raging whirlpool of thoughts.

Reflecting on his walk, the things he'd seen and heard, Cypress felt in his soul a profound mixture of awe at nature's relentless reclamation and sorrow for humanity's plight. The charm of the rewilded city was undeniable, but what a great cost it came at; he thought of the people he had seen struggling to adapt, the pain and desperation that had taken root in the absence of almost everything humanity had come to depend upon.

He lay there until the sky faded to pink, then orange, then a shimmering black; he gazed up at the stars, struck by their sheer brilliance. The tyrannical neon lights that once dominated the skyline without mercy were gone, unveiling a glowing collage of galaxies and constellations he had never seen before. The sky, now a vast expanse of glittering jewels, filled him with a sense of wonder and melancholy - amidst the sorrow, a small spark of gratitude began to flicker within him. The simplicity of this new world, the raw beauty of the untamed wilderness, was changing something within him too.

For the first time in years, he felt truly connected to the world around him, unencumbered by the noise and distractions of modern life. As he lay bathed in the glow of starlight, he found himself quietly thankful to whatever, or, as some deep-rooted instinct told him, *whoever,* was behind it all.

As Cypress lay there, lost in his thoughts, he heard the soft rustling of grass beside him. He turned his head and saw a woman he reckoned to be a little taller than himself, settling down next to him. Spirals of curly blonde hair framed her face, contrasting with her tanned skin, and bounced onto the grass away from her pale blue eyes and full lips as she lay down.

"Mind if I join you?" she asked, her soft voice tinged with the weariness of recent tears. "I just need some company."

He nodded, offering a faint smile. "Of course."

The woman introduced herself as Havana, and as Cypress returned the gesture she took a steadying breath before speaking again. "My husband, Atticus... he passed away last week," she began, her voice cracking slightly, and Cypress found himself wondering if it was the first time she'd managed to say the words out loud. "We'd only just about been married a month. He had a heart condition and couldn't get his medication after everything fell apart. That, along with the stress... it was too much."

Cypress felt a pang of sympathy and instinctively reached out, taking her hand in his. She allowed him, and squeezed his hand in return, her grip firm but gentle, seeking solace in the simple connection.

"I'm so sorry," he murmured, turning to face her, his own eyes reflecting the sorrow in hers. "The world has changed so much, and not all of it for the better."

Havana nodded, her gaze drifting up to the stars. "I just don't get it," she sniffed, absentmindedly pulling up blades of grass from next to her and throwing them into the darkness. "How did this happen? How is there suddenly just... nothing?"

"I feel like some part of me *does* get it," confessed Cypress, taking his own chance to say the words he'd been holding onto out loud. "I mean, I don't. But somehow I feel like I should. I know that don't make no sense, but I'm telling you, there's something..."

"You're looking for meaning where there is none, Cypress," Havana told him tenderly, her fingers caressing the back of his hand. "We all are. We all want to understand what's going on, because to lose understanding is to lose all control. And on some level, we're all control freaks by nature."

"Maybe you're right," he mused. "I just feel like there's something right there, right at the back of my mind, you know? It's driving me crazy. It's like when you hear a few bars of a song, and the lyrics are right on the tip of your tongue. But you just can't find 'em, and the rest of the song goes unsung."

Havana squeezed his hand tighter. "It's been a long time since we heard any songs, apart from the people busking outside. And the word song would have to be used damn loosely for most of those."

"They'll find a way," Cypress said as Havana shifted herself closer to him, draping a tightly toned arm across his body. He stroked her platinum curls, determined to give her the illusion of far more confidence than he really had. "We'll all find a way. I promise you."

Secretly, it was a promise to himself, too.

And he intended to keep it.

CHAPTER EIGHTEEN

In the weeks and months that followed, Belial's holy army of roots and vines continued their merciless advance, determined to choke out and swallow the evils of the modern world.

The city had now completed its full transformation into a vast, sprawling garden. Grasses, bushes, and fungi spread like wildfire, carpeting streets and infiltrating abandoned buildings at an alarming rate. Cypress walked along what had once been a bustling avenue, now a leafy tunnel shaded by colossal bushes that had seemed to appear from nowhere one night; he noticed a group of people gathered around a huge, leafy bush, their hands moving deftly as they inspected its pinkish-orange berries. Approaching quietly, he joined them, watching as an elderly woman carefully plucked a handful of the small, round fruits.

"These are safe," she said, her voice calm and authoritative. "I think they're red huckleberries. I've been eating them for days now - they're a bit sour, but they'll keep you going."

The citizens of New York City, much like those in every other part of the world, had been left to figure out which plants they could eat, which they could feed their pets and children, through an often vicious process of trial and error.

A voice of knowledge meant a rare moment of security, and so a murmur of relief spread through the group as they began harvesting the berries, their movements quick and efficient.

Cypress picked a berry and cautiously tasted it, the tartness bursting on his tongue. He joined the harvest, quickly pawing handfuls of fruits into the basket he'd used in what felt like a different lifetime to sell his paintings on the Square, where they tumbled down on top of mushrooms, stonebaked bread rolls, and various other soft fruits - the results of the morning foraging and trading venture that had taken the place of grocery shopping.

Content with his bounty, he turned towards home, preparing for the twenty-nine-storey hike to his apartment. When he finally reached his personal summit, he opened the door and smiled at the sight of his new lodger sitting cross-legged on the floor, tongue sticking out slightly in concentration as she daubed various shades of green, yellow, and red on a small round canvas.

Havana and her husband, so she'd explained, had a vast collection of country music CDs - the music died first, when the destruction of electricity extinguished the stereo, but they'd still had each other to sing and talk to. Now, in the deafening silence left behind when nature claimed him too, she couldn't face being home alone, so Cypress had invited her to stay the night. The night turned into the week, and she'd quickly made herself at home in his bed, while he consigned himself to the sofa.

Hearing the door handle, she looked up and grinned. "Thanks for letting me use some of your paints." She looked down at her creation, her broad smile fading into a more apologetic one as she took in its naïve kindergarten-finger-painting charm. "I know I'm not doing very well... I won't waste any more, since we don't know if and when you'll be able to replace them. But I've enjoyed using them!"

Cypress placed the basket on the counter and sat down on the floor next to her.

"Art is whatever you need it to be," he told her softly. "It doesn't need to be photorealistic - hell, anyone can take a photo. Not every photo can make someone feel something. And seeing what you've created... that makes me feel something, for sure."

She wrapped her arms around him in a hug before jumping back when she realized that her hands were splattered with lime green paint. "When I see you painting that shit out there - the plants - you know what it makes *me* feel?" she whispered. He shook his head, silently inviting her to continue. "It makes me see the beauty in them. I don't see the monster that took Atticus from me. I don't see the death, the mess, the destruction of everything I've ever known. I see the colors, the animals, the life. And I hate it so much less."

"Is that why you wanted to try to paint it, too?" he asked, reaching out to twirl one of her curls around his finger.

"Yeah," she muttered. "I guess I wanted to try to make it beautiful, too."

"You *do*, Havana," he assured her. "Everyone has a way of

making things beautiful. Some people can sing like a nightingale, so nice that they make you forget about all the cruel words and cryin' in the world. Some people can highlight the beauty in an ugly world with a paintbrush. And some people - and they're the best of all - they can make the world more beautiful just by existing in it. Like rainbows! You know how rainbows come out after the rain, and they just shine so pretty that it makes the rain worth it? That's you. You're a rainbow. You don't need to be the next Picasso after four hours to make this world beautiful - your presence does that all by itself."

She looked over at him, her eyes full of charged emotions and unspoken words. Her breath hitched for a moment, then she leaned over to kiss him; a tentative, gentle peck on the lips. He hesitated for a moment before reciprocating, pulling her closer, feeling her heart pound in time with his own pulse pounding in his ears.

The softness of her lips against his ignited a warmth that spread through his chest as his hand found the small of her back, anchoring her body to his as if he was afraid she might slip away as swiftly and unexpectedly as every other aspect of their lives had. The kiss deepened, each touch more certain, more fervent, becoming a silent conversation of fears, hopes, longing, and comfort, until their bodies were one.

Later, as they shared red huckleberries from Cypress' basket, both still clad only in a giddy afterglow, Havana looked at him, her eyes brimming with sadness and curiosity.

"I spoke to the woman downstairs yesterday," she

breathed. "The baker - the Cuban lady."

"Rita?" he asked through a mouthful of berries, and she nodded in reply.

"She loves me, 'cause she thinks I was a sign. She said that her parents arrived a few days after I did."

"From Cuba?" he asked, confused. "How? There ain't no planes. They come by boat?"

"From *Havana*, specifically. That's why she thinks I'm the Messiah, I guess. But here's the thing," Havana continued. "They didn't arrive normally - you know, show up with suitcases at the door. Rita woke up to make breakfast for her husband, husband was just... gone. She's convinced he's in Cuba, with his mama - he'd been talking about how he wished he could go home. And sleeping in their bed when she runs back to the bedroom looking for him are her parents."

"What the f-" Cypress started, but Havana wasn't finished.

"What if I wake up tomorrow and you're back in Texas? And everything is gone, again, and I'm alone listening to my own damn breaths and thoughts all day. I can't do it again." Her voice cracked, and the tears welling in her eyes finally spilled over, trickling down her cheeks.

"It sounds like people are somehow waking up where they want to be, or at least where they're s'posed to be," he reassured her. "Of course I miss my family, I even miss Texas at times, but they'll be okay. They got a cattle ranch and a big-ass allotment, nobody's going hungry down there, so that's why they ain't showing up in New York - last time they saw it, it was all bright lights and concrete. Plus, we ain't all that close. Maybe one day we'll find a way, but for now I'm good. I'm in no rush to go anywhere that's not with you. Okay?"

She nodded with a weak smile, laying her head back down on his chest. "I wonder how it's happening," she said quietly, perhaps to herself more than to Cypress. "This all gets weirder by the day. I don't get it."

"I still feel like I do," he replied, earning a scoff and a light-hearted eye roll from Havana. "I'm dead serious. It's like I read about it, or dreamed about it, maybe. Heck if I know. All I know is that I know, or *I knew,* something."

Before she had a chance to respond, their conversation was interrupted by a sudden outburst of yelling outside. Since the bars closed and the cars stopped working, this kind of commotion in the streets that was once part of daily life had become rare, and the pair jumped to their feet, pulling on their clothes as they ran over to the window.

Looking down at what had once been a bodega, they saw a man Cypress recognized as its owner - a bearded man in his mid-fifties - and his three teenage sons. One of the boys was accompanied by Dayanara, who had evidently succeeded in finding company, and they were joined by an assortment of unfamiliar faces in what appeared to be a small mob. Armed with axes, fire extinguishers, and kitchen knives, they hacked and chopped at the vines and leaves that coated the bodega, screaming their frustrations into the open air.

Cypress felt a surge of anger jolt through him. The sight of the plants being destroyed, the sheer violence of it, made his blood boil for reasons he couldn't quite explain. "I need to go down there," he said, turning to Havana. "I can't just stand here and watch 'em do this."

Havana grabbed his arm, her eyes wide with fear. "Cypress, no. Jesus, they're armed. I can't lose you in the name of this madness too."

He looked into her powder blue eyes, touched by the desperation and worry he found there. He hesitated, torn between his desire to protect the new life sprouting around them and the need to keep himself safe, keep *Havana* safe from further loss.

As they stood there at an impasse, Cypress noticed a group of people beginning to gather at the corner of the street. He squinted, recognizing one of them; it was Asher, the young man he'd seen working in the community garden. He was accompanied by several others, all of whom looked determined and focused.

"They're here to stop them, you can stay here," Havana sighed, unable to mask the relief washing over her features.

Cypress watched as Asher and his group approached the angry crowd. Asher, leading the pack, held up his hands in a gesture of peace and called out to them: "Hey! What do you think you're doing?"

The mob paused, their angry shouts faltering, as Cypress slowly and carefully opened the window to hear the exchange more clearly. The bodega owner, his face glistening red with exertion and rage, turned to face Asher. "What do you care, kid? This nonsense is taking over everything! We can't live like this!"

Asher took a guarded step closer, his voice calm and steady. "We can find a way to live with them. Destroying them won't solve anything. We need to work together, find a balance. The plants are part of the city now, they live here, just like us."

Dayanara stepped forward, her ax hanging limply at her side in a bizarre opposition to the soft floral frills of her sundress. "So, what are we supposed to do? Just let them take over? *They took my fucking dad.* Do we just lay down and accept that?"

"We *adapt*," Asher told the girl firmly. "We learn from each other. We find new ways to survive, to thrive. This anger, this violence - it's only gonna result in more loss. It won't get you anywhere."

The mob began to waver, their anger dissipating as they listened. The bodega owner lowered his santoku knife, the fight visibly leaving his body. "Alright," he said gruffly. "Fine. I'll give it a try. But if it doesn't work, we won't just stand by and let this happen."

With mumbles and grumbles of reluctant approval, the mob dispersed, but their simmering resentment loomed in their wake like a storm on the horizon. In the stillness they left behind, a silent promise lingered in the air: the real fight was yet to come.

CHAPTER NINETEEN

When the storm came to shore, it was a tempest, the likes of which most had never seen.

Small skirmishes flared up more and more often, sparking like brushfires between those desperate to return to the status quo and those committed to preserving the new natural world. The people had split into two camps, gathering to plot in abandoned buildings and once-bustling parks, now overrun with greenery, where the air was now thick with the sharp scent of anger and fear.

The pro-tech faction, armed with the remnants of their technological past, shouted their cause from rooftops and street corners. They called themselves 'technomancers', determined to bring technology back to life; they argued that without it, humanity was doomed to suffer from preventable diseases and conditions.

Leading technomancers pointed to the rising death toll of those who could not access their necessary medications, to the mothers dying in childbirth, and to the children who had once thrived with medical interventions now gasping their last breaths.

For them, technology was not a matter of simple convenience; it was the key to survival, a lifeline brutally severed.

On the other side, the pro-nature advocates, reclaiming the title of "rootbound" given to them by their opponents, stood firm in their belief that the world was simply healing. They saw the rampant technological advancements as the true harbinger of death, poisoning the air, the water, and the land, and they openly rejoiced in their demise.

The rootbound argued that the old way of life had been a slow, inevitable march towards extinction; to them, nature's reclamation was a necessary reset, a chance for humanity to live in harmony with nature, ensuring the survival of not just themselves but all life on the planet.

The clashes between the two factions grew more violent as time went on - verbal confrontations evolved into fistfights, then into armed struggles, and before long, the city streets were battlegrounds. The greenery that had overtaken the concrete jungle now bore the scars of human conflict: uprooted plants, broken branches, and blood-stained leaves lay strewn across the ground. The sense of community that had briefly flourished in the aftermath of the world's transformation was now a distant memory, replaced by a bitter divide that seemed insurmountable. And the final confrontation loomed large overhead, an inevitable clash that would later be known as the Battle of Reclamation.

As its shadow descended, King Belial and the Fae folk watched on in morbid fascination from the other side of the veil.

Diogeneia, one of the oldest of the naiads, though her appearance had remained that of a young maiden for as long as the water she cared for could remember, shook her head in sorrow as she watched the reflection of the conflict in the glassy surface of her spring. "If we could change their world so much, so quickly, surely we can do something now," she asserted. "Isn't it our duty to make it right?"

Two rocksprites known as Gabbro and Granophyre looked on from the embankment, their coarse, grayish skin and pebble-like eyes blending in almost flawlessly to the gravel around them. "You know what humans do if they see two street cats fightin' in an alleyway?" rasped Gabbro. Diogeneia, knowing that the question was rhetorical, did not respond outside of a pensive nod.

"They leave 'em alone," explained Granophyre, taking her silence for confusion. "Pull 'em apart and both cats'll turn and scratch the shit out of *you*."

And so the alley cats were left alone, and in Times Square, once the pulsing neon heart of the city, the conflict finally reached its grisly zenith.

Technomancers clad in improvised armor fashioned from salvaged electronic parts advanced on the square with grim resolve. Those who did not have guns proudly carried makeshift weapons - spiked metal rods, shards of glass, and sputtering drills seemingly powered by desperate energy and ferocity alone. The final sparks and arcs of electricity spewed from their devices as they fought, the acrid smell of burning circuitry mingling with the thick smoke that poured from damaged electronics, every movement punctuated by the screech of malfunctioning equipment and the stench of burning plastic.

The rootbound camp fought them with primal strength and unwavering determination; they wielded weapons carved from wood and stone, jagged rocks and sharpened bone, a testament to the strength of the natural world they guarded. Their faces were set in fierce concentration, hardened by the urgency of the fight. The ground beneath them churned and buckled, with dirt and debris flying in every direction as they clashed with their opponents.

The scene descended into one of raw, unfiltered violence, where the air was thick with the pungent stench of burnt technology and the earthy smell of blood and sweat. Smoke billowed from the scorched remnants of electronic devices and burned plants, creating a choking haze that obscured vision and stung the eyes as sparks flew from shattered circuitry, and as it cleared, one could easily wish it hadn't as they saw that the ground was littered with teeth and hair among the fragments of twisted metal and splintered wood.

The technomancers' initially imposing barricades of scrap metal and old wiring were being torn apart, their defenses crumbling under the relentless assault of the rootbound; metal shields were battered and buckled, and makeshift fortifications were reduced to heaps of debris. The clanging crunch of metal on metal reverberated through the leaves that coated the city's streets, and the rootbound fighters, though equally battered, fought with the same dogged perseverance as the plants they were prepared to give their lives for. Their weapons struck with crushing force, shattering the technomancers' equipment and sending sparks and debris flying.

The technomancers' desperate cries were swallowed by the cacophony of combat as pools of dark, oily fluid mixed with the crimson of spilled blood. Torn and battered bodies lay scattered amidst the wreckage of their aspirations, the brutal clash leaving an indelible mark on the urban landscape.

It was no longer a mere battle for survival; it was a reflection of a grander struggle, a tug of war for the very soul of a world teetering between old and new. As nightfall draped its dark cloak over the battlefield, the struggle raged on with an unrelenting fury, each side fueled by their convictions and desperation, and by the time the first light of dawn cast its pale glow across the battlefield, both factions had swelled their ranks with fresh reinforcements.

Emerging from the overgrown leaf tunnel that once housed the hotels and restaurants of 44th Street, a young woman appeared on the battlefield, an unexpected sight amidst the chaos. Dressed in a shell-pink rockabilly dress that swung around her knees and matching ankle boots, her hair a shambolic patchwork of various shades of peach and magenta, she stood out vividly against the war-torn landscape.

Unfazed by the ruination before her, she strode forward, her boots making soft thuds against the ground, until she reached a female fighter with blood-matted hair and a deep scratch down her face. The fighter was furiously wildly pulling up plants at the tunnel's opening, and the woman in pink grabbed her arm, trying in vain to drag her away.

"Stop, " she cried, her voice cutting through the cacophony. "Please, Naomi, just- *stop that!*"

The technomancer, momentarily taken aback by hearing her name, paused. "Milla? Camilla Jenkins?"

"Yeah! Yeah, it's me," Camilla said, her wide eyes imploring the elfin redhead in her grasp to listen. "Look, I know it sounds crazy, but after you dropped out of college I went to work for Matt Bellisle. The day before this happened, he came and told me how to dye my hair if I couldn't get hold of regular dye - I mean, it didn't work too well, but my point is: I *know* he had something to do with this, or at least knew it was gonna happen."

At that, Camilla felt a firm, claw-like grip on her own left shoulder and released the other girl, spinning around to face the person behind it. She found herself facing a wild-haired, wild-eyed woman shorter and thinner than herself; a carbon replica of Naomi except perhaps three years older, her previously neon-colored ensemble now marred with mud and blood. "You're telling me *you* worked for the bastard behind all of this?" the woman snarled.

"Zip, leave it," yelped Naomi, placing herself between the two. "I know Milla. We hung out all the time in freshman year, before I dropped out to look after Mom. She's cool."

"Cool? Naomi, she's rootbound," hissed Zip. "There's nothing cool about excusing what's going on here, much less working for the ones calling the shots. So, *Milla*, tell me - what exactly do you know about Matt Bellisle, and where is he now?"

"All I know is he's a good man," Camilla pleaded. "There has to be more to this than we understand…"

"A good man?" roared Zip. "My mother lost her life two weeks in because her insulin meter stopped working along with everything else. How could the one who killed my mom be *a good man?* How could the person who let us all plunge headfirst into this hellscape without a whisper of warning possibly be *a good man?*"

She pushed her younger sister out of the way, leaving her sprawled on the floor, and grabbed a fistful of Camilla's thick, bushy hair. "I'll give you one more chance to tell me where your sugar daddy is," she spat. "I lost a friend because I didn't believe him that some weird shit was going down. You know whose name popped up in that conversation? Mr. Bellisle. And now I lost my mom, and everything I had, and lo and behold, his name pops up again." Her grip tightened, making Camilla wince in pain. "Either you tell me where he is so I can kill him, or I kill you instead."

"I promise you, I don't know where he is," she grimaced. Naomi, having swiftly regained her footing, struggled desperately to pry her sister's hands away, attempting to free Camilla from her sister's fierce clutch. Her efforts, however, proved futile; with a sharp squeal of pain, Naomi recoiled as her older sister, once a vivacious party girl who cried for the mice on the glue traps in the basement of the coffee shop she worked in, sank her teeth into her hand. The bite left deep, sharply lined indentations, stark against her skin, turning desperation to panic as Naomi realized the true depth of her sister's frenzy.

"Zipporah, I'm begging you, don't hurt her," she howled, frantically trying to reach the soft heart she still believed to be inside. "If she says she doesn't know, I believe her. She doesn't know where he is. Let her go, Zippy."

Zip paused for a moment, her breath coming in short, jagged bursts, and slightly loosened her grip on Camilla's hair. Camilla slowly adjusted her position to relieve the strain on her neck, acutely aware that any wrong move could prove mortally dangerous. As she did so, she locked eyes with Naomi, whose relief was visible on her scarred face, and allowed herself to release the breath she'd been holding.

"See, she's not doing anything," pleaded Naomi with a forced smile. "Let go of her hair, sis. She's not hurting anyone."

"She said the bastard who did this, or at least knew it was coming and didn't warn us, was a good man. He told her how to dye her stupid cotton candy hair, and not how to *save lives*. This little bitch's hair was more important to him than people's lives - more important than Mom. That hurts *me*," explained Zip, her voice eerily calm.

"I understand that," said Camilla. "I'm sorry about your mom. I really am. If I knew her, and knew how to save her, I would have, I swear. If I knew even half of what was really gonna happen, I'd like to think I would have found out how to save people like her, but I didn't. I only knew what Mr. Bellisle told me, and that was... how to dye my hair with lemons and beets. I'm sorry, okay? I didn't know, and I sure as hell don't know what to do now."

"Good thing I do," smiled Zip, untangling her hand from the younger woman's hair.

"You... you do?" asked Camilla warily, eyeing Zip with skin-crawling suspicion. Still, she spotted the jagged shard of metal in her hand too late, and before she could scream, or beg, or flee, it was lodged in the hollow of her throat. Her eyes grew wider as her hands fumbled in the air, trying to grasp it, but instead she crumpled to her knees before falling flat on the ground, her weight driving the metal scrap deeper.

"That one goes out to you, King Belial," Zip screamed to the sky. "I know you're out there somewhere. Will you face me now?"

She looked down at Camilla's body, a nauseating chill striking her in the chest as she looked at the pool of blood seeping from beneath the girl, her lifeless eyes, the fearful expression frozen on her face. Her sister, Naomi, knelt beside her motionless friend, tears flooding down her face as she retched, choking on the air she so wretchedly wished she still shared with Camilla, with her mother, and with the sister she'd lost to madness.

Zip turned her eyes back to the sky, tears stinging at the corners of them. "Don't let her die for nothing," she said, her voice far quieter now, hoarser. *"May God strike you if you don't face me now."*

CHAPTER TWENTY

As Zip stood, glowering with fierce determination at the clear blue sky, she felt movement around her feet. At first, she dismissed it as the tickle of grass, but the sensation quickly intensified. She looked down, eyes widening in shock as she spotted her assailant; thick brownish-green vines, sinister and sentient, were snaking around her ankles with alarming speed.

Before she could react, the vines yanked her to the ground. She landed hard on her bottom, the impact jarring her spine; she tried to scramble backward, her hands clawing at the earth, but the vines only tightened their grip, constricting her ankles and calves with steady pressure, effortlessly binding them together.

Some of her fellow technomancers ran to her aid, but they were deftly slapped out of the way by green tendrils. Screams pinged through the crowd, panic surging through both sides of the battlefield, but none more so than Zip as she struggled against her constantly tightening restraints. She kicked out wildly, cursing and spitting at the vines, but it was no use. The vines were unyielding, and eventually, with a stomach-turning pop, her ankle jolted out of place, sending a wave of searing pain up her leg.

Zip screamed, the sound raw and primal, filled with a mixture of fear and rage.

She clawed at the ground, desperate to free herself, but the vines only tightened their hold as her struggling grew weak and her breaths turned into ragged gasps. The pain in her ankle was unbearable, her body trembling with the effort to stay conscious, when she saw a spectral figure walking towards her.

She would have thought him a hallucination were other people not clambering over each other in fear, technomancers and rootbound alike, hiding behind each other as they watched his approach.

Easily nine feet tall and draped in a flowing mantle of leaves, he approached with a grace that belied his immense size. A living crown of roots and flowers adorned his head, each bloom and tendril shifting subtly with his movements. His skin was a pale, softly shimmering green, contrasting with the misty, creamy white of his hair that cascaded down his back. His eyes, entirely white and devoid of pupils, seemed to bore a hole in the very core of her being.

"My Lord?" she shivered, gazing up at him with a mixture of fear and awe.

"Not quite," he replied in a voice far softer than she had expected. "But allow me to clarify this first, Zipporah: I have no fear of your Lord, nor of you, and he has no will nor right to strike me for not doing as you ask. I do not take kindly to threats. Is that clear?"

Fear crashed over Zip like a bucket of ice water as she

realized who she was looking at.

"Belial?"

"The very same," he replied. He gestured with a strong, long-fingered hand, and at his silent command, the pressure on her ankle began to subside. She watched as the vines uncoiled themselves, releasing her legs, though her alabaster skin still bore angry red marks where they had been. "Stand," he commanded.

"That's gonna be a little difficult, seeing as your crazy grass ropes yanked my fucking ankle out of its socket," Zip snapped, before immediately turning apologetic at the sight of Belial's affronted expression. "I'm sorry. It's just… my mom. Then I… I *killed a woman.* And now I don't know how I'm gonna fix my ankle because I can't just call a doctor, can I? And it's all because of you."

Without another word, he bent down and effortlessly lifted the redhead from the ground, his touch surprisingly gentle despite his immense strength. Zip's breath caught in her throat as he set her back on her feet.

To her astonishment, the pain she anticipated as he set her down never came. She stood there, wobbling like a newborn fawn, feeling the ground solid beneath her and watching the vines retreating as if in deference to Belial's presence. Tentatively, she took a step and then another, marveling at the absence of pain. A combination of awe and trepidation filled her as she stared up at Belial, who watched her with an inscrutable expression.

Her anger and fear were still markedly present, but mingled

with them now was a newfound curiosity as she realized fully, for the first time despite the palpable strangeness and danger of this new world, that there were forces at play far beyond her understanding.

"Not because of me," the king declared solemnly. "As readily as I may have taken the blame for centuries, I refuse to do so this time."

The silent huddles of people began to move carefully toward him, creeping through the wreckage. Each step was cautious, their feet barely disturbing the littered ground beneath them, and the air was thick with tension, every breath shallow and measured. As they moved, the plants around them began to stir, their leaves rustling with a soft sussuration, the sound reminiscent of whispers shared in secret.

The vines and leaves raised themselves from the ground like cobras, uncoiling with a slow, deliberate grace. They interlinked and twisted together, forming a colossal, organic podium. The creaking of the plants echoed through the air, the victory cry of a planet reclaiming its power. Belial ascended with the rising structure, lifted higher and higher until he towered above the gathering masses.

From his elevated position, he looked down upon the people, his white eyes surveying the scene with an otherworldly calm. The crowd's movements were almost imperceptible, a collective shift as they drew closer yet, drawn by a mixture of awe and fear. The podium of vines continued to grow, branches and leaves braiding themselves together to create a throne befitting the king of nature.

Belial stood tall, his mantle rustling in the breeze, a living testament to the power that now held sway over the world. The people below him seemed insignificant in comparison, their clustered forms dwarfed by the sheer magnitude of the natural and supernatural forces at play.

"Allow me, first, to introduce myself," he boomed, his voice carrying through the crowded battlefield. "Some of you may have heard my name - some may hold it in high regard, others in contempt. Many will never have heard it at all. My name is Belial, King of the Fae, Lord of the Earth."

The people below him remained frozen, staring upwards. Families huddled together, scared for their lives. "Please don't be afraid," Belial continued, though it did little to ease the collective terror on the ground. "I am here to explain why nature has reclaimed your world, and why it had no choice but to do so."

His voice grew louder yet, seeming to swish on the wind through the leaves, drawing growing numbers of citizens to the tattered square to hear his speech.

"You stand in the first dawn light of a new era," he told the crowd.

"Now, this may not be an era you have consciously chosen, but it is one that has been thrust upon you by the merciless selfishness of your own actions. We, the ancient ones - demons, gods, Fae folk, and other beings of old - watched and waited for perhaps too long, hoping that you would hear the earth's cries and change your ways. Please believe that we tried to save you without such... extreme measures.

We whispered warnings in the winds, sent omens through the tides, and delivered messages through the cracks of lightning in the sky. But each cry of the earth - each tidal wave of tears, each howl of the wind, each angry strike of lightning - was ignored. You turned a blind eye to the very signs that were meant to guide you.

For centuries, I have looked on as you exploited my kingdom, taking more than you needed from my forests, leaving scars on the landscape and poisons in the waters. You not only ignored every sign from the earth herself, but refused to pay any regard to explicit warnings from the news, from academics, from activists who sought to protect your future. Your relentless pursuit of material and comfort has come at a great cost, not only to the world around you but to your own souls.

I will confess that our intentions are not entirely selfless. The ancient ones need your interaction, your energy, to survive. In your stories, you have always known this, yet you dismissed us as myths, as relics of a forgotten past. But we are real, and many of us are bound to you. When the earth suffers, we suffer. When you perish, so do we. And so, to save both your lives and ours, we were forced to take action.

This action has led to the world you see now - a world where nature has reclaimed its throne, where technology and money have been stripped away. This was not done out of malice, but out of necessity. The earth could not endure your neglect any longer, and neither could we. The balance had to be restored, and in doing so, we have given you a second chance."

The air seemed to hum in time with his words, the plants around him rustling in agreement.

"I ask for this mindless fighting to stop. Instead of destroying each other over what has been lost, I implore you to work together, learn to move forward without the technology and power that once defined your existence. Embrace nature as your lifeline, for it is through harmony with the natural world that you will find your true strength. The earth is resilient, and as her children, so are you.

We, the ancient ones, will help you as much as we can. Already, we have ensured that separated families wake up together, reuniting loved ones who thought they had been lost forever. We will continue to offer our guidance and support, but you must be willing to listen, to learn, and to adapt. See, you may not have heeded the earth's calls for help, but I will heed yours. And so will many other powerful beings who have already walked among you secretly, offering aid in ways you never realized. We are here to help you heal, to help you grow, and to help you find a new way of living that respects and honors the natural world.

Because this is not the end of your story, but a new beginning. It is an opportunity to rewrite the narrative of humanity, to forge a path you can survive on. One that is just, and filled with hope instead of greed. Do not squander this chance. Embrace it with open hearts and minds, and together, we can create a world where both nature *and* humanity flourish."

He paused, allowing his words to sink in, watching the faces of the people, seeing the dawning realization and guilt that many had begun to feel. His voice softened, still carrying with it the sorrow of ages of lost opportunities.

"You must ask yourself, do you wish to continue to fight against the inevitable, clinging to the remnants of a world that no longer exists? Or will you rise to the challenge, embracing the new reality and working together to build a better future? The path forward is not easy, I admit. But it is one that you must walk. And I assure you once again that we will be with you every step of the way.

Take this moment to reflect on what truly matters to you. Is it the technology that once enslaved you, the money that so many wasted the best years of their lives chasing only to reach the other side of the veil alone and without purpose? Or is it the natural world around you - the world that now offers you a chance at redemption? Does your loyalty lie with the fleeting comforts of the past, or the promise of a harmonious future? The answers are within you, and you know them well.

So let this be the dawn of a new age; an age where the lessons of the past guide you toward a brighter, more sustainable future. An age where the ancient ones and humanity work hand in hand to heal the wounds of the earth and build a world that is truly worth living in.

The journey will be long, and the challenges will be great. But together, you can, and will, overcome them. You can create a world where both nature and humanity thrive. It's time to end the violence and embrace this new beginning, and let us - human, nature and spirit - move forward as the united force we were always meant to be."

As the final echoes of Belial's speech began to fade into the warming mid-morning air, a profound silence enveloped the crowd. The words of the king had resonated deeply, stirring something in the hearts of those who had gathered. For a fleeting moment, the relentless tension and fear that had pervaded their lives seemed to lift. The weight of their struggle, the bitter losses, and the uncertainty of the future were, at least momentarily, overshadowed by a glimmer of hope.

The applause started hesitantly, with a few scattered claps, but quickly gathered momentum as more people joined in. The sound swelled like a wave, rising and falling in a rhythm of collective resolve. Faces softened, eyes brightened, and the earlier confusion and frustration were replaced with a tentative but undeniable sense of unity.

Of course, the chasm was not entirely bridged - amid the wave of agreement and newfound hope, not everyone was ready to let go of their grievances. A few technomancers, their expressions set in stubborn defiance, continued to voice their displeasure. Their cries were punctuated with anger, their voices high and raw, but they were quickly swallowed by the larger consensus that had formed. They spat curses and shouted accusations, their anger directed at an invisible enemy, but their efforts to disrupt the mood were in vain. The crowd's focus remained firmly on Belial, and their willingness to embrace this new chapter was evident in their actions.

As the applause began to dwindle and the crowd started to disperse, a slight man emerged from the middle of the assembly. His long dark hair fell untidily around his face, and his movements were apprehensive, marked by the visible discomfort of an injury. His arm, clearly broken, was bound in a makeshift sling fashioned from brightly patterned silk.

The man moved with a deliberate, slightly unsteady gait, his tired hazel eyes fixed firmly on Belial. The weight of his injury seemed to momentarily dissolve in the face of an overwhelming realization. His voice, though tinged with a strain of pain and exhaustion, carried a clarity and conviction that cut through the remaining murmurs of the crowd.

"I know you!" he called out, his voice cutting through the ambient noise of the dispersing crowd. "I know you, King Belial! Or should I say *Matt Bellisle?*"

CHAPTER TWENTY-ONE

King Belial's gaze shifted as the words cut through the air, the spiritual air of his presence growing even more pronounced. He looked down, his white eyes locking onto the slender form of the man who had called out his name. The corners of his lips curled into a faint, knowing smile.

"Well, hello, Mr. Rafferty," Belial smiled, fond recognition radiating from his voice. "What a pleasant surprise."

The sound of his name spoken by the ancient being struck Cypress like a freight train, triggering a flood of memories that surged through his mind with overwhelming force. He staggered, grabbing a stunned Havana's hand to steady himself. His breath felt coarse in his throat as images from his past whirled wildly in his mind; flashes of his early encounters with demons, the adrenaline rush of observing Paimon, the gravity of his first meeting with Belial, the chilling terror that had gripped him when confronted by Belphegor and Beelzebub. Faces, voices, and places blurred together, forming a jigsaw puzzle of experiences that had shaped him in ways he had long forgotten.

As the memories cascaded through his consciousness, Cypress's hand instinctively moved to touch the silk supporting his broken arm.

The vibrant patterns and the soft texture brought a sudden clarity, grounding him in the present. He remembered the eccentric street merchant who had recognized him, the kindness in their eyes as they tied the makeshift sling.

His gaze darted around the crowd, searching with a newfound urgency. "That was-" he gasped in awe and disbelief.

Before he could finish, a familiar presence sidled up alongside him. "Yes, dearie," Paimon said, their voice dripping with a peculiar blend of affection and mischief. "That was yours truly."

Havana, having come to her senses, gripped her partner's hand tightly. "What's going on, Cy?" she asked, her voice trembling.

"I…" Cypress faltered, burying his head in the crook of her neck. "I don't know where to start, baby bird."

"Forgive the intrusion, darlings, but perhaps I could help with that?"

Paimon stood with a scarf in their hand, cornflower blue with shimmering white threads resembling clouds. Cypress understood, and with a labored breath, uttered his consent. The djinn draped the scarf over his head, then placed a supportive arm around Havana as they instructed her to pull it off.

"Why?" she asked warily, and Paimon responded with a calm tenderness that instantly eased the shaking of her hands.

"If you want to understand, honey, that's the easiest way. It's how I made him forget everything he knew about the other side of the veil - because he asked me to, just to clarify that. And if you unveil him, you unveil his secrets. That means everything you need to know about him, you'll know."

"Best hope he's not keeping any other secrets, then, huh?" she laughed nervously. Then she pulled. His memories played like a video montage in front of her mind's eye, and she collapsed backward into the waiting arms of Paimon.

"Havana!" cried Cypress. "Baby bird? Are you okay?"

"She's just fine," confirmed Paimon as her larimar eyes fluttered open. "She's in shock. You'll still need to fill in a lot of gaps, but she's got the gist of it. Right, sweetpea?"

"You were right," she croaked, looking at Cypress, dumbfounded. "You always said that some part of you felt like you should understand all of this. Like you knew the song, but forgot the lyrics. And - oh my God - you were right. *What?*"

Before Cypress had a chance to respond, he heard another voice calling his name. Turning around, he saw Mialani, his former girlfriend, pushing her way through the remaining flocks of people to reach him. Her coarse hair was no longer in her signature cornrows, but rather cropped short, peeking from beneath her cap. Cypress also reckoned she'd lost fifty pounds since last time they saw each other; most of the rounded curves he'd known had been whittled away by stress and the travail of finding food in this new world. Still, he recognized her instantly.

"I owe you one hell of an apology," she told him. "I'm so, so sorry for how I treated you when you told me. I can only imagine how much it must have hurt to be told you were lying or crazy when you were holding onto all of that. My girl passed out back there listening to that, Ulysses had to carry her into the shade, she's still tripping out."

Taking in Cypress' questioning look, she laughed. "Sorry, I guess you missed a few chapters. When I told Apollonia that we broke up, she took the chance to tell me she was in love with me, and, well, the rest is history. My point is: she nearly lost her mind just seeing that big green dude and the plants moving around, here with me and all these other people. You… you carried that shit alone. You knew, and you trusted me to share that burden with you. And I wouldn't listen. I don't know if I can forgive myself for that, but I hope at least you can forgive me."

Cypress took a deep breath, filled with both gratitude for the acknowledgment and a deep sense of empathy for Mialani. He realized that if someone had told him, before the reclamation began, the same things he had told her, he would have dismissed them as the ravings of a crazy drunk too.

"It's okay, Lani," he reassured her. "You weren't to know. I ain't got nothing to forgive. I'm happy for you and Apollonia, and I'm glad you knew peace for a whole lot longer than I did."

"Can I ask you one thing?" she said quietly, and Cypress nodded.

"Why didn't you try to prove it? Try to force me to see it?"

"I want the people I care about to be happy and healthy," he explained. "If I'm not part of that, and especially if I think I might turn into part of the reason why they're *not*, I'll step aside and let 'em thrive without me. Keeping 'em around is like keeping a firefly in a jar. I wasn't about to watch you lose your shine for my sake."

"I appreciate that," she said. "But that means you've just been walking around since then, knowing all of this was happening because of some demons, not telling anyone because they wouldn't believe you? Because I didn't believe you?"

Cypress let out a short burst of laughter, startling her. "Heck, no, I'd have lost my marbles. I had no idea. Would you believe me if I told you that a demon king made me an enchanted scarf that erased the whole thing from my brain? As far as I knew, you just left because I wasn't making time for you. Vegas was an uneventful vacation. And all of this - with the plants - was as odd to me as it was to you."

"You know what? I do believe you," she said, and he could tell that she meant it. "Holy shit... I don't know what to say except, again, I'm so sorry."

"I'm sorry too."

Cypress and Lani both turned to face the source of the tearstained voice. Havana stood bowlegged, still clinging to Paimon to stay on her feet, red-eyed and sniffing.
"I should have listened. Maybe we could have figured it all out together," she told him through tears. "I just laughed at you."

"No, no, baby bird, don't think like that," he pleaded, pulling her from Paimon's arms into his own. "You did absolutely nothing wrong. And nor did she." He gestured at Lani, who shuffled her feet, watching them awkwardly.

"Sorry, I'm being rude here - Lani, this is my girlfriend, Havana. Havana, this is Lani, she's…"

"His ex," interjected Lani. "Had to rip off that band-aid, sorry. But it's all good - you're more my type than he is these days, if you get me. I'm Mialani Torres, Lani for short." She offered her hand with a mischievous grin, and Havana stepped forward and shook it, giggling.

"Well, that's reassuring… I think," she smiled back at the younger woman. "Havana Dove. It's a pleasure to meet you."

"The pleasure's all mine," said Lani, miming the gesture of tipping her baseball cap. "Real talk, though - are you okay? You don't look okay. This is a lot to take in."

"I'm not sure, honestly," Havana admitted. "I was made a widow at thirty-three. I lost my purpose, too - I was a cybersecurity analyst, then suddenly there's just no need for me in the world, overnight. I don't know where most of my friends ended up. And now there's this. Demons? I did some work on the computer systems in Bellisle Tower, for God's sake - now I find out he's… *that?*" She gestured to Belial, who now walked in stoic grief through the debris of the battlefield. "And the serial killer who got one of my late husband's friends was a demonic owl? And that's not to mention poor Cypress - no. I don't think I am okay."

Her voice wavered, and Cypress placed a protective arm around her waist. She turned toward him, inhaling the scent of his hair before continuing. "I'm not sure how I *can* be okay. But I will be, and so will Cy. And you and your girlfriend, too. It's just gonna take time."

"You got that right, girl. *A damn long time,*" Lani concurred, before excusing herself to tend to her own shellshocked partner.

In the same moment, not sixty feet away, King Belial approached the lifeless form of the girl who'd once served as his intern. He gently turned her onto her back, removing Zip's makeshift blade from her body. With a flick of his wrist, the bloodstained metal was gone, replaced by a spray of blush-pink pear blossom flowers that fell over Camilla as he closed her eyes for the final time with his fingers.

As he lowered himself to his knees, speaking quietly over her in a tongue as old as time, he felt a presence in his space. He looked up to find Zip watching silently, the skin around her eyes angry and puffy from crying. She was biting her lip in an attempt to hold back a new flood of tears, but as Belial's eyes met hers, it came forth anyway. "Can you bring her back?" she wept. "She wasn't hurting anyone. She was innocent. She didn't deserve to… to…"

She broke into loud, bitter sobs, unable to bring herself to say the last word.

"To die?" said Belial. "No, she did not. But if we reversed death every time we considered it an injustice, the wheel of fortune would simply stop turning, the cycle never complete. What is dead must stay dead, and return to nature to bring forth new life. I'm sorry, Zipporah. She cannot, and will not, come back."

"Her family-" the young woman wailed, stricken with rue.

"Her family will have the chance to say goodbye," the king promised, rising to his feet. "I will make sure of that, personally."

And he who was once known as the Lord of Lies stayed true to his word.

That same evening, under the new woodland canopy near the moss and mushroom-coated Brooklyn Bridge, a gathering of heavy hearts took place. King Belial, with an air of noble sobriety, led Camilla Jenkins' parents, grandparents, and nine-year-old sister to a secluded corner. The Fae had already prepared her for the journey to the afterlife, wrapping her body in gossamer and grasses in a sacred Sylphic burial ritual. The delicate wrapping extended up to her chin, concealing her fatal wound and leaving her face peaceful, as if she were merely asleep.

Both sets of grandparents approached her first. With their hands clasped together, they murmured prayers to a God they clung tight to their faith in, their voices a soft, trembling hum that blended with the whispers of the surrounding leaves. Their prayers pleaded for peace and protection, asking their deity to guide Camilla's spirit safely to the other side and take care of her as she awaited their arrival.

Her parents stepped forward next, their faces etched with sorrow and gratitude. "Thank you," her mother said, her voice cracking as she turned to Belial. "She always spoke so highly of you. Thank you for taking good care of her, in life and in... departure." Her father nodded, unable to find words, his eyes glistening with unshed tears. They each placed a gentle kiss on her forehead, lingering for a moment before stepping back.

Cosette, a cherubic girl with strawberry blonde pigtails, approached last. She gazed at her sister with wide, innocent eyes, her small hand reaching out to touch Camilla's pink hair. "Goodnight, Milla-Wafer," she breathed, her voice barely audible. She stroked her sister's pink hair tenderly, mirroring the way Camilla would caress her to sleep after a nightmare.

When she moved away, back to the arms of her father, Belial approached with his uncrowned head bowed. He lifted Camilla effortlessly and gently laid her into the waiting earth; her parents, determined to see her burial through, tried to help him to fill in the grave. They scooped earth over her with shaking hands until they could bear it no longer. Unable to watch as her face was covered, they turned away, their shoulders shaking with silent sobs.

Belial continued the task with quiet dignity, his movements steady and deliberate. As the last handful of soil was placed, the woodland itself sighed, the leaves softly playing a mournful song that Camilla's soul itself seemed to sing along to.

In the fading light, the family huddled together, finding solace in their shared grief. They lingered for some time, sharing stories about Camilla's life and tales of her dreams for the future. When Cosette, exhausted in every way, started to fall asleep on her mother's shoulder, they moved towards the bridge with occasional pained glances back, finally heading for home.

As they disappeared from sight, Belial turned his eyes to a particular willow tree, seemingly identical to every other one in the woodland. His gaze lingered, as if he could see beyond its craggy bark, perceiving the hidden presence behind it. Then, with a weary sigh, he finally spoke. "You can come out now," he said, a soft mix of resignation and understanding behind his words.

From behind the tree, a waiflike redheaded woman emerged, her lip bloody from where she had been anxiously biting it. Her hands were wringing together, knuckles white from the tension. Her eyes, wide and filled with remorse, darted nervously as she approached Belial, her steps hesitant and faltering.

"I'm sorry," Zip choked out, her voice trembling. "I just wanted to see them… oh, God, the little girl. She loved her so much. What did I do?"

Tears welled up in her eyes, spilling over as she spoke. She took a tentative step closer to Belial, her body shaking with the force of her emotions. The sight of Cosette's innocent face as she said her last goodnight to her sister, the raw grief of the whole family, had torn apart something deep within her soul.

Belial regarded her with sorrow, but also with compassion. He could see the torment in her eyes, the realization of the consequences of her actions eating her from the inside out. The silence stretched between them, heavy with unspoken words, as Zip struggled to find her footing in the wake of her own contrition.

"You took a sister, a daughter, a granddaughter," he said matter-of-factly. "A friend, a first love, a sworn enemy, perhaps. You took something from many people, and everything from one."

"What am I supposed to do?" she asked quietly, looking up at the king with pleading eyes. "If I go with her, I'm taking everything that I am away from my loved ones, too. But how do I just carry on now? How do I live with what I've become?"

"What you've done is not the same thing as what you've become," Belial told her. His expression grew gentle, and he extended a hand toward Zip, a gesture of understanding and an offer of redemption. "Come with me."

She placed a trembling hand in his, taken aback by its sheer size and bracken texture. She let him lead her through the quiet grove until they reached the freshly turned earth marking Camilla's final resting place, but faltered at its edge, pulling back.

Belial released her hand and opened his own, revealing a delicate seedling with writhing roots, yearning for the earth. "*Dombeya Burgessiae* - a pink wild pear blossom tree," he explained. "She asked me to put a picture of one on her office wall. I wish I had. She loved them - she loved everything pink."

Gently, he scooped away some of the earth with his hand. He placed the seedling tenderly into the ground, and covered its roots, patting down the soil with the care of a father tucking his child into bed for the first time.

"I want you to return here as often as you can. Water this tree, prune its leaves, care for it in every way and watch it grow," he instructed Zip.

"The only way to restore the balance in your soul is to help bring forth new life from the one you took."

Zip gazed down at the fragile seedling, silently vowing to tend to it for as long as she lived, and from her eyelash fell the first drop of water to grace its soil.

CHAPTER TWENTY-TWO

As that one little seedling began to grow and thrive in the aftermath of devastation, so, too, did the world outside its woodland.

The new dawn Belial had promised quickly broke into day; people moved with a sense of purpose and unity, embracing the symbiosis between themselves and their environment. Even those who once called themselves technomancers, so fiercely opposed to nature's takeover that they had given and taken lives in resistance, now turned their attentions to replicating what had been lost using the boundless resources around them.

In the heart of the transformed city, on the very ground where the Battle of Reclamation had raged, massive clusters of bio-composters now stood guard. The enormous mushroom formations, some rivaling the height of the old buildings that once dominated the skyline, had become vital workers in the new world. They presided over the land in timeless service, their intricate network of mycelium sprawled beneath the surface like the tentacles of an earthbound Kraken, devouring old food and sewage. And they did not merely consume waste; they transformed it, breaking it down into rich, fertile soil.

Soil that, teeming with the vibrant essence of life, became the bedrock upon which the people grew their food; fruits, pulses and vegetables. Each mushroom honcho now stood as a silent supervisor of this era of harmony, their towering forms a testament to the renewed balance between humanity and nature. Their very existence, after all, was a reminder of the cycle of life, where waste fed the earth and the earth, in turn, fed the world; a delicate dance of renewal and decay that now sustained the world.

And as those who'd been engineers and scientists in another lifetime managed to craft devices from salvaged materials, a new thing began to grow in the soil: hope. The citizens watched on as people in dusted-off protective suits began the intricate process of capturing the gases released by the bio-composters.

With care, they guided the gases through a network of makeshift pipes and filters, channeling them into dull, scratched glass tanks. Then, from those tanks, the captured energy was directed to a series of old streetlights, their sleeping bulbs now waiting for a wake-up call they thought would never come. As dusk settled over the city, anticipation rippled through a gathered crowd. When the first light flickered on, its glow spreading in a warm, golden hue, a collective gasp swept through the onlookers. Some people began to cry, overwhelmed by the sight of the simple streetlight illuminating the darkness after so many years of shadows. Their tears fell shamelessly, splashing into the joy and disbelief of the moment.

Yet, as quickly as the light cast its soft radiance on the streets, it faded again.

Despite the disappointment that rippled through the crowd, there was an unspoken agreement among them. The collective promise, voiced through resolute silence, was to never attempt to return to the old ways. The light, brief as it was, had symbolized a new beginning rather than a return to the past. It was a reminder of their resolve to move forward and embrace the new world, illuminated by the promise of possibility.

Other people found other uses for the abundant resources around them. In his studio, Cypress spent most of his time experimenting with natural colors. He created vibrant colors from crushed berries, flower petals, leaves, minerals; whatever he could find. He had long run out of traditional canvases, instead finding their purpose in old television and computer screens. Though useless for their original purposes, these screens, with their flat, blank surfaces, became perfect ground for his art.

He painted scenes of the new world and the old; some people loved the vibrant colors of forests reclaiming the urban landscape, while others wanted reminders of the neon lights and bustling traffic that came before. His works adorned the homes of those in the community, their old devices traded back to them with a new lease of life in exchange for food and clothing.

Meanwhile, Havana had long abandoned her attempts at painting, instead discovering the beauty of the plants through their practical potential. Her analytical mind reveled in uncovering new possibilities hidden between their roots and leaves, aided by no end of knowledge from beyond the veil.

Belial had kept his promise. The ancient ones now walked openly among the people, assisting where needed - though for the sake of peace, most continued to veil their true appearances, blending in seamlessly to the eyes of those who didn't seek them. When Havana first asked Paimon for help finding new potential in the plants, they'd introduced her to someone seemingly entirely unassuming. A very short, angular man peered at her over his glasses, his sharp features and intense gaze softened somewhat by a small, knowing smile.

"Prince Stolas," he said in a plummy English accent, extending a hand. He explained that he had no end of knowledge of alchemy, plants and stones, gathered by painstakingly studying them for over a hundred thousand years.

Havana blinked, processing the information, and was surprised to find she was unfazed. The world had changed so much that even meeting a prince of the underworld who walked among her cave-dwelling ancestors simply felt *normal.*

"Havana Dove. So, you're here to help me?" she asked, curiosity piquing her tone.

Stolas nodded. "To help all of you. I'm assisting people around the world in gaining knowledge of the natural resources around them. We are writing books to ensure new medicines can be invented, treatments replicated without chemicals. The natural world holds countless secrets, and it is high time we unlock them."

He gestured to the plants around them, his eyes twinkling

with a profound understanding.

"Take this, for instance." He plucked a leaf from a vine twisted around a traffic light, holding it up to the sun. "This leaf contains properties that can soothe pain, if prepared correctly. And the root of this little beauty- " He bent down, pulling a small bristly plant from the earth "-has been used for centuries in the treatment of fever. The knowledge was lost to many with the rise of modern pharmaceuticals, but we can bring it back."

Havana nodded, absorbing his words. "And you're... teaching people how to do this?"

"Yes," he replied. "Not alone, mind you - I govern twenty-six legions of spirits, most of whom are gifted in the same field I am. We are seeing to it that nature schools and workshops are set up everywhere, to help the people make the most of the new world."

A sense of purpose filled Havana since her office had fallen silent that first day, her computer screen never to light up again. She looked at the plants around her with new eyes, seeing not only their potential but her own. "Thank you, Prince Stolas," she smiled earnestly. "This means more than you can know."

And so, with the help of Stolas' ancient helpers known as the Gaians, she rediscovered herself and the world around her, blooming quickly and beautifully into a new role as a waterwarden.

Waterwardens created plant-powered water filters, using aquatic plants grown to purify water. The plants thrived in

New York's once murky ponds and the vast Hudson River, who had long been choked by the waste of old factories and city grime. They worked tirelessly, their roots drinking in the dross and transforming the tainted waters into crystal-clear oases for drinking, cooking and bathing.

And Stolas was not alone in helping the fresh new world to flourish. Even the most unexpected of allies, once thought lost to the veiled realm forever, emerged to lend their aid.

It was much to Cypress' shock that he discovered this fact. It was an ordinary Thursday morning. He walked to the vegetable garden, whistling back to the birds, a painting of a pink wild pear tree in blossom on an old flatscreen television tucked under his arm. But as he approached the kindly woman who agreed to trade a basket of her prized tomatoes and a loaf of zucchini bread for the artwork, he stopped in his tracks.

A tall, spindly man in a pinstripe suit leaned languidly against the tomato trellis, large round sunglasses giving him a bug-like appearance.

"You-" gasped Cypress, pointing in disbelief at a face he never thought he'd see again.

"Me," grinned Prince Beelzebub, removing his glasses to meet the shorter man's eye. "Don't worry, I come in peace this time."

Sensing that Cypress was unconvinced, he continued: "I'm here to guard the tomatoes - well, all of the crops, everywhere, really, but Mrs. Jenkins pays me well in sweet treats to take extra care of her toms. That was my job once before; my role in this world. I chased the flies away from crops, and in return, I received food offerings. It's been a *looong* sabbatical, but here I am. I'm back, baby!"

Cypress' eyes widened as he took in what Beelzebub was saying. "That's why they call you Lord of the Flies? You have the power to make the bugs pollinate the plants, or leave them alone? Oh, that's why you're associated with food too! It all makes sense! I always thought..."

"That I was associated with flies and food because I'm greedy, dirty and worthless? Yeah. You and just about every other person in the world. You know, I hated that more than the whole Satan thing. At least the Satan stuff was a nice ego boost; being likened to a fly by the very people who created traps, sprays and so many other ways to kill them? When I used to be the one they asked for help? That was no fun at all. Imagine spending thousands of years helping people, only for them to sneer at you, demonize you and compare you to the very problem you'd once helped them solve." His voice shook with what may have been anger or sadness; he'd have claimed it was neither, though Cypress suspected it was both.

"I'm glad that people see the truth now, and *without* me having to start any goddamn cults," Cypress winked.

Beelzebub returned the wink before returning his sunglasses to his eyes. He pulled Cypress' basket from his hand and took it to Mrs. Jenkins, a slim lady in her sixties whose strawberry blonde hair was slowly fading to the color of straw itself. Cypress watched, awestruck, as he observed not a *demon* but an *ancient deity of agriculture*, guiding her liver spotted hands towards the biggest, sweetest tomatoes and helping her place them gently in the basket.

When they were done, Cypress handed the painting to Mrs. Jenkins before taking the basket from Beelzebub. "Thank you both," he nodded. "I hope I did your late daughter's favorite tree justice."

"It's beautiful," she smiled sadly. "It would have been her birthday this weekend. She always wanted a picture of one of these trees; now she has one as a birthday gift, thanks to you. You're a good man."

"Thank you, ma'am. I try to be," said Cypress, before turning to Beelzebub. "On that note, it was nice to see you in better circumstances."

"Better circumstances? You hurled a can of beans at my brother's face last time I saw you. It doesn't get much better than that," smirked the Lord of the Flies. "Nonetheless, it's my pleasure to meet you again, too."

And that's how the world ticked along, for a while.

The people lived alongside the ancient ones, learning from them, relying on their wisdom and power, exploring the folds of a veil that had never been thinner. On the other side, the balance was restoring itself too, with the ancient ones finding true meaning and purpose in their own existence for the first time in centuries.

King Belial often stood at the window of what had once been his office, now his palace while he was on the mortal side of the veil. One day, as he stood watching the people gathering food, teaching their children about the various crops and the pollinators that buzzed around them, a blinding beam of sunlight flooded through the window. The glow engulfed him completely for a second, and he knew he was not alone.

"Emperor," he acknowledged as a vision in white stepped silently out of the light, watching from the window alongside him.

"When I gave you my blessing, I told you that I wished the winds of fate to be at your back," Lucifer told him. "Since then, society has begun to rebuild, growing alongside your vines. Families and communities are blossoming like your wildflowers. The babies being born into them are raised in a world they respect, with knowledge of those on both sides of the veil who made it what it is. The winds of fate blew strong, old friend, and regardless of how close you came to being shipwrecked along the way, you made it to shore with your spirit unbroken."

Belial straightened his posture and allowed himself a barely perceptible smile.

The helm had been stiff, and splintered his hands, but it had been worth it.

He'd made it to shore, with the world as his crew.

And the horizon had never looked brighter.

EPILOGUE

THE CENTENARY OF THE BATTLE OF RECLAMATION

In the hundred years following the Battle of Reclamation, the scars faded, and the earth rediscovered her rhythm.

Though King Belial and the other ancient ones had long since returned to the veiled realms, their presence was felt more keenly than ever. Their power, now widely acknowledged and believed in, remained a guiding force, providing help and wisdom when needed.

What once was new became old, and what was old became new as primitive inventions got a second chance to flourish. Horses and camels once again became the primary means of transport, their hooves and padded feet a familiar sound in lively villages and sprawling fields across the world.

Among the children, technology and money were now seen as distant, malevolent entities that had once nearly destroyed the world. Stories of power and inequality, of lives dominated by material greed, were whispered by parents as cautionary tales, warnings to never repeat the mistakes of the past.

In New York City, a young girl, just days from her ninth birthday, skipped along a dirt path lined with wildflowers. She and her mother were on their home from Thyme Square, a thriving garden of life that had once borne a different name and been the site of a grim battle to the death, following the centenary commemoration.

Her eyes sparkled with curiosity and innocence, her white-blonde curls bouncing around her shoulders as she skipped. Suddenly, she turned to face her mother, who walked behind her, and said with a hint of defiance: "I don't think I even *believe* in the battle, mama. It all sounds like monster stories, not real things."

Her mother smiled fondly, a mixture of pride and nostalgia in her gaze. "I want to show you something when we get home," she said. "I think it's time."

"Come *on*, then, mama, let's go quickly," begged the little girl excitedly, pulling her by the hand.

The two ran home, both as excited as the other to share the moment ahead. When they got there, the mother pulled an untitled brown book from a cluttered shelf on the wall; its leather cover was tattered, clearly well-loved, and she stroked it fondly.

"This book," she said, handing it carefully to her daughter, "was written by my great-grandpa. He was there during the first attempts to appease materialism. And in some tiny way, he was part of the reason things changed."

The girl's icy blue eyes widened with awe.

"Is it really true?" she asked in a whisper, her fingers tracing the worn edges of the book.

"It sure is," her mother nodded. "Look."

She helped her daughter to open the book, pointing out the name written neatly inside the front cover. "See? Cypress Rafferty. Just like your great-grandma - my Nanny, who I named you Belle after. Her full name was Bellanita *Rafferty*-Dove, Cypress was her dad.

Her mom, Havana, did the actual writing; apparently she couldn't get up and down the stairs too well while she was pregnant. So she stayed home, he told her his story while he painted, and she wrote it down.

They gave it to your great-grandma Belle to read when she started asking questions. Then one day she gave it to Grampy, and he gave it to me. And now it's yours."

Belle breathed out a gentle *"Whoa!"* and turned the page, her small hands trembling slightly with excitement.

"The simplest explanation is probably the right one," she read aloud, carefully sounding out the syllables in the longer words. "Occam's Razor - a principle that I swore I'd stick to all my life. Until I couldn't. Because it made sense. Until it didn't."

Printed in Great Britain
by Amazon